A TALE OF TWO BODIES

WATERFELL TWEED COZY MYSTERY SERIES:
BOOK TWO

MONA MARPLE

For A

My inspiration, my reason why

"*Y*ou've outdone yourself!" Sandy said, after a few moments of making appreciative noises as she sampled Bernice's latest cake creation.

"Do you think?" Bernice asked.

"It's far too nice." Coral agreed, taking another bite of her own sample slice. "This won't be any good for my hips."

The three of them were standing in the kitchen of Books and Bakes, Sandy's bookshop and cafe, hiding out from the crowds for a few seconds on a busy day.

The upstairs bookshop had been open for six weeks and, as Sandy had hoped, it had transformed the business. While her cafe remained a popular haven for the villagers themselves, people flocked from far and wide to see her lovely books.

"Hello? Is anyone serving?" Someone called from the counter. The three glanced at each other and laughed and Sandy and Coral returned out front, leaving Bernice to finish decorating her new cake.

"Sorry Dorie." Sandy said, not surprised to see her most

regular customer standing at the till. Dorie was small and round with hair like candyfloss.

"Don't let this success go to your head, you still need to look after your best customers."

"You're right," Sandy said. The best way to handle Dorie was to agree with her. "What do you fancy? Do you want to sit down and I'll bring it over?"

Dorie looked around her from side to side, as if scared her cake order would be overheard. "I actually need a book, could you help me find the right one?"

Sandy laughed. She had dreamed of her days being full of requests like that ever since she opened the shop. "Of course I can. Coral, mind the till while I go upstairs with Dorie."

She lead Dorie to the back of the coffee shop, through the small section of downstairs books. She'd extended the cafe area a little when she extended into the upstairs space but had kept some of the most popular books on the ground floor too. Things like children's books and local interest stood with pride to catch the cafe visitors' eyes.

The upstairs was larger than the downstairs. Sandy had thought it was a trick of the mind when she first saw the space, but her landlord Ignatius Potter confirmed her suspicions.

It was a beautiful space, renovated with a careful hand to keep the original wooden beams. The windows had been replaced throughout the years but kept as similar in character to the original sash windows as they could. While he was an eccentric man, it had to be said that her landlord cared about the appearance of the village. All of the properties he owned - and there were plenty of them - were managed in a similarly sympathetic way.

"Here you go, Dorie. Are you after something in particular?"

Dorie had visited the cafe almost daily since it had opened, and usually alone. She'd never bought a book in all of that time.

"It's a present." Dorie said, glancing at the bookshelves as Sandy paced the length of the upper floor with her.

"Who for?" Sandy asked.

"That's a personal question." Dorie scolded.

"It will help me suggest ideas if I know who we're looking for," Sandy said, surprised by the woman's secrecy. Dorie was the biggest gossip in Waterfell Tweed.

"It's a gentleman," Dorie admitted.

"Ok," Sandy said. It would be Dorie's son, Jim. The two of them were very close. "How about a nice leather journal?"

"Oh no, no, I don't think so." Dorie said.

Sandy continued walking through the aisles, wondering what Jim would appreciate as a gift. It was a momentous occasion, a local wanting to buy a gift from her bookshop, and she needed to get it right. Dorie trailed behind her, appearing uncomfortable around so many books.

"What about this history of the police force?" Sandy asked. Jim was a local police constable. According to Dorie, he ran the whole of the local police force.

"Don't you have anything more exotic?" Dorie asked. "Travel? Something like that?"

Sandy returned the police book to the shelf and turned on her heels towards the travel section. She had a large collection of coffee table books with beautiful photography inside. "They're all here, anywhere in particular?"

Dorie examined the titles without standing too close to the bookcase. The woman's awkwardness around books made Sandy have to stifle a laugh.

"Africa." Dorie said, after a few moments.

Sandy pulled out a large hardback and held it open for Dorie, flicking through the pages to show her the photographs contained within. "This is a really nice one."

"Hmm." Dorie murmured. "Would a man like it?"

"I think so," Sandy said. "Well, I mean, the right man would. An intelligent, stylish man."

"I'll take it," Dorie said. "Will you wrap it for me and I'll get myself a coffee?"

"Of course," Sandy said. "You go down and I'll bring it to you."

There was a small till in the far corner upstairs, and while gift wrapping wasn't strictly a service she had planned to offer, it surprised her how many people requested it, so she had kept a selection of wrapping paper behind the till. The till itself was usually not manned, with all customers being served at the cafe till downstairs, but as the shop grew increasingly busy, Sandy expected she would have to man the upstairs till full-time soon.

"Excuse me?" A voice called as she worked at wrapping Dorie's book.

Sandy glanced up to see a man standing in front of her. His hair was bedraggled and his trousers were worn and dirty. He carried an old, and bursting full, bag for life in his right hand. "Can I help?"

"Go'a job?" The man asked, stepping closer to Sandy. She stepped back before she realised she had. The man noticed and stepped back himself, putting more space between the two of them.

"Excuse me? A job? I haven't seen you around before." Sandy said although she knew that was a silly comment. He didn't appear to have any money to allow him to be a regular visitor for coffee and cake.

"I ain't been around before. Just looking for a job, lady, nowt else." The man said, holding his hands up as if Sandy had accused him of having a gun.

"I... erm... I haven't got any jobs at the moment, I'm afraid." Sandy said. "I can offer you some lunch, though, if you'd like?"

The man eyed her. "Your customers wouldn't like me down there with them."

"That's not true," Sandy said although it was. Waterfell Tweed could be an old-fashioned village, and many people's opinions on homelessness were not that nice. "But I can get something brought up here if you'd prefer."

"Nah lady, don't worry. All I need's a job." The man said, already walking away. Sandy watched him, saw how he lingered over the aisles as he walked away, stopping to touch books. He picked up an illustrated poetry anthology and ran his fingers along the cover.

"Wait, what's your name?"

"Anton. Anton Carmichael." The man said, without turning back to her.

"Give me a second," Sandy instructed, picking up Dorie's wrapped book and scurrying past the man and down the stairs. The cafe was bustling, and both Coral and Bernice were taking orders and serving up food. Sandy slipped behind the counter and picked up a brown bag, then selected a large slice of chocolate fudge cake for it. She pulled a loaf of bread from beneath the counter and sliced two thick doorstep slices, slathering them in butter and adding lettuce, plenty of bacon, and tomato. Then, she sliced the sandwich in half and placed that in another brown bag, and made a large coffee in a takeout cup.

"You're not having your lunch now, are you? We're manic!" Coral called, whizzing past her with a single dirty plate. Coral was brilliant front of house with customers but her ability to balance the dirties needed work.

"No, don't worry, this is for someone else." Sandy called as she walked through the busy cafe area and up the stairs.

A few people were milling around the bookshelves, some with stacks of books piled high in their arms. The sight of her book stock being enjoyed always made Sandy's heart swell.

"Anton?" She called out, peering in each aisle. She looked for him in travel and topography, in science and self-help, in children's and cooking. He was gone. Finally, she stood by one of the sash windows that overlooked the village square. It was raining, it had been all day, and the temperatures were approaching freezing. Just as she was about to give up, she saw a scruffy figure of a man walk past the butchers and then disappear from view.

She gave a deep sigh and returned downstairs.

"Are you ok?" Bernice asked, noticing Sandy's face as she returned to the kitchen.

"I think we've just had a homeless man in," Sandy said, standing at the counter and still looking out of the shop window.

"Did he steal anything?" Dorie called. She was sitting at her usual table, polishing off a sausage sandwich.

"No!" Sandy cried. "He wanted a job, actually."

"That's what they do," Dorie said. "It's called the cover. They get you talking, lower your guard, and then take what they've been eyeing up."

"That's very judgmental, Dorothy." Sandy scolded.

"My Jim told me, so it's not judgmental, it's a police-corroborated fact," Dorie said, her posture straightening with pride as it always did when she spoke about her son.

"She's right," Bernice said. "We all need to be more careful, there's more crime now."

Sandy rolled her eyes. Apart from the murder of Reginald Halfman, the village had remained it's usual, crime-free, sleepy self. "What crime?"

"There's so much rubbish," Coral said, and Sandy couldn't argue with that. The village square was unusually messy, it had to be said.

"I'm not sure that leaving rubbish is a huge crime, and that could be the teenagers. They're always loitering around waiting for the bus."

"It's the squatters," Dorie said, chewing her last mouthful of food. "Lovely sandwich as always."

"What squatters?" Sandy asked.

Dorie sighed. "For a woman so involved in the community, you don't pay enough attention to what's happening."

"She's got a point," Coral said. "Everyone knows about the squatters."

"I've been busy," Sandy said in exasperation, and it was true. She had bootstrapped the extension as much as she could, and that had meant moving all of the books herself, buying the bookshelves at auction and assembling them herself, painting the upstairs herself to freshen it up, and giving the upstairs carpet a shampoo treatment - herself. "Will someone tell me what you're all talking about?"

"The Manor's been taken over by homeless people, they're squatting in there," Coral said. Although she had left her journalist career behind her to come and work in the cafe, she still enjoyed breaking headline news when she could.

"The Manor? Are you serious?" Sandy asked. Waterfell Manor was home to the Harlow family, wealthy and generous benefactors of the village. Following their daughter's arrest for murder, Benedict and Penelope Harlow had announced they would be leaving the village for some time to spend time with their son, Sebastian, who was travelling the world.

"It's an awful business," Bernice said, her voice quiet. Bernice, like Sandy, was not one for village gossip.

"Surely the Manor wasn't empty, though? What about the staff?" Sandy asked. The Harlows had employed a team of staff, including a full-time housekeeper.

"There's only Pritti, the others were hired as needed," Bernice said.

"I don't understand how this could happen," Sandy said. She was fond of the Manor house, it was such a part of the village.

"Word spreads among these people," Dorie said.

"Excuse me for a moment," Sandy said. She sprinted up the stairs, thinking of Dorie's certainty that Anton Carmichael would have been in the shop to steal. Sandy darted through the bookcases until she reached the poetry section, her heart beating in her chest until the familiar pattern caught her eye.

She pulled out the anthology that Anton had been looking at earlier.

It was still in perfect condition.

2

*S*andy was going to spend a rare evening at The Tweed. The village's pub rarely offered much more than cask ales and a roaring fire, but the landlord had announced his plans to try out a quiz night.

It had been a hectic day in Books and Bakes, and Sandy would have preferred to be changing into her pyjamas and curling up with her latest novel, but she didn't like to let people down.

By the time she pulled up outside her cottage, her sister Coral was standing on the doorstep.

"I'm sorry!" Sandy called, as she parked up. She locked the car and unlocked the door, letting Coral enter first.

"What happened in here? It looks like a bombsite." Coral said, looking at the piles of clothes laid out on the settee.

"I'm having a clear out," Sandy said. "I haven't worn any of these clothes for years."

"I'm not surprised - size 10!" Coral laughed, holding up a pair of tiny jeans. "When were you ever a size 10?"

Sandy felt her cheeks flush. "I got those to motivate me when I was trying to lose weight."

"Ah, that old trick. Never worked for me." Coral said, tossing the jeans back over the settee. "Anyway, you're fine as you are."

"I know," Sandy said, and she meant it. Her body was wobbly in places, but she didn't let it bother her.

They were disturbed by a knock at the door. Sandy padded back into the hallway and opened the door. In the few moments that she had been inside with Coral, it had started to rain.

"Awful weather!" Her best friend, Cass, exclaimed, darting in the house. Her sister, Olivia, stood behind her, biting her thumb nail.

"Come in, Olivia, don't get wet." Sandy said. She had spent a few evenings with Olivia since her arrival in the village, but didn't feel like she knew the girl yet. She had initially thought she was sullen, but realised that she was actually painfully shy. She reminded Sandy of herself as a teenager; awkward and self-conscious.

"Evening!" Coral called. She was examining the rest of the pile of clothes, looking at each item before tossing it down.

"It's pouring down out there," Cass told her. "I'm not driving, I need a glass of wine after this week. Ooh, these are nice."

"I'm having a clear out," Sandy said. "Help yourself if you want anything, any of you."

Cass joined Coral in examining the clothes, while Olivia hung back by the door.

"These look brand new," Cass said, holding up the pair of jeans that Coral had already examined.

"Never quite right for me," Sandy said, with a smile.

"They're nice." Olivia's little voice came.

"Take them," Sandy said. "You'd be doing me a favour."

Coral eyed her but said nothing.

"Shall we get going or have a drink here before we set off?" Sandy asked, as Olivia moved into the room and joined Cass in looking through the clothes.

"If we stay here for a drink we'll never make it out the house. Let's go." Coral said.

"Ok, well I'll drive. I'm only drinking mocha in this weather anyway!" Sandy said.

The four of them piled into her old Land Rover and made the short drive to The Tweed, finding a parking space on the road nearby. They sat in the car for a few moments after they had parked, none of them too keen to open the doors and get wet again.

"I wish you'd lived in the Bahamas, or somewhere," Olivia whispered to Cass in the back seat. Everyone laughed.

"Waterfell Tweed is beautiful," Cass said, her bright pink lips bursting into a smile. "Wet, and windy, but beautiful."

"Come on, we can't hide out here all night," Coral ordered, and the four doors opened. The women all broke into a run, bursting into The Tweed with such force that the landlord looked up from pouring a pint.

"All right, ladies?" Tom Nelson asked.

"Better now we're dry!" Sandy said with a laugh. Tom nodded and returned to serving.

The pub was busier than normal, but there were a few tables left. Coral lead the group to a booth near the fire, and they all removed coats and sat down.

"Love your dress," Cass said to Sandy. Cass was very interested in clothes and make-up, while Sandy didn't have much time for those concerns. It was surprising that the two had been best friends for so long, considering how different their interests were. While Sandy was devoted to her bookshop and cafe, Cass ran a nail salon, and there was no better example of their different interests.

"I think you bought it for me," Sandy said, with a laugh. It was a 1940s style dress which ballooned out in the skirt. She'd had it for a few years but didn't have much chance to wear it.

"Yes!" Cass exclaimed. "Didn't I get a matching one? You should have said and we could have matched!"

"I'm so glad you didn't," Olivia mumbled and everyone laughed.

"Drinks?" Coral asked, already standing up. She was always the leader in a situation, even if all it came down to was organising a group of women to order their drinks.

"I'll have a mocha, please. In a big mug, if Tom's got one." Sandy said, passing a few pound coins across the table to her sister.

Coral and Cass both ordered wine, and Olivia asked for a hot chocolate.

"How's school been?" Sandy asked Olivia.

Olivia groaned.

"Don't listen to her," Cass said, her eyelids fluttering under heavy coats of mascara. "She came home on Monday buzzing about it. And she's done her homework every night without being asked."

"Yeah, it's alright I suppose." Olivia agreed. Maybe there was a part sullen teenager to her after all, Sandy thought to herself.

"What's your favourite lesson?"

"English, but when I choose my college classes I want to do law," Olivia said, her cheeks burning with a self-conscious heat.

"Law? Do you want to be a lawyer then?" Cass asked, the revelation coming as news to her too.

Olivia nodded.

"What kind of lawyer? You can do all sorts with law."

"I'd like to do human rights," Olivia said, her voice a whisper.

Sandy and Cass looked at each other and raised their eyebrows in surprise. Olivia had had a tough life, being removed from her mum when she was a young child and placed in care before running away to find the sister she had never met.

"That's amazing," Sandy said, reaching over and giving Olivia's hand a squeeze. Olivia looked at her and smiled.

"Well, we'll do everything we can to help you," Cass said, although her expression gave away her concern.

"Help with what?" Coral asked, returning to the table with the glasses of wine. "He's bringing the hot drinks over."

"Nothing," Olivia said, returning her gaze to the table. Sandy shrugged at Coral, who knew enough about teenage girls to let it go.

"Here we are ladies, a hot chocolate?" Tom Nelson asked, appearing at their table.

"Yes!" Olivia said, raising her hand as if she was in class.

"And the mocha must be yours, Sandy, nobody else drinks these."

"Really?" Sandy asked in surprise. She loved nothing more than a mug of hot mocha.

"Nah, I only buy the sachets for you. And I used the biggest mug I could find." Tom said. Sandy looked at him and felt herself blush. He was a fine looking man, tall and muscular. He returned her gaze and met her eyes for a moment longer than was comfortable.

"What was that about?" Cass asked as soon as he moved away from the table and returned to the bar.

"What?" Coral and Sandy asked in unison.

"You and The Hunk! Since when do you have chemistry with Tom Nelson?"

Sandy felt her cheeks burn. "Keep your voice down, Cass, I don't need any rumours starting like that. I don't know what you're talking about."

"He is a hunk," Coral said, taking a sip of her wine.

Olivia screwed her face up in disgust.

"I think he'd have asked you on a date if we hadn't been here." Cass said.

"Don't be silly. I've known Tom for years." Sandy said, although to her surprise, when she looked up at the bar, Tom was looking right at her. He grinned and then returned to his work. And Sandy's stomach did a flip of excitement.

"We've all known Tom for years, but he's on the market now."

"Is he?" Sandy asked, trying to sound more nonchalant than needed which had the opposite effect. Although she had known Tom for years, she only knew him to exchange pleasantries with. He never visited the cafe and she rarely visited the pub, unless she was catering a wake, so she couldn't call him a friend, let alone a close friend.

"Did he get rid of that awful woman?" Coral asked.

"That's what I've heard," Cass said. "And it seems he's ready to move on. What a catch he would be."

"The quiz will start in five minutes, please make sure your table has a Team Name!" Tom's voice came booming out through a microphone.

"Oh no," Cass said, looking past Sandy to the front door. "Don't look now."

Sandy did what anyone told not to look would, and turned around to look. To her surprise, the young man who had admired the poetry book in her shop had walked in the pub. He looked bedraggled, and his clothes were soaking wet. He spoke to each table for a moment, finally reaching their own.

"Can ya spare any change?" He asked, not making eye contact with them.

"No, you shouldn't be in here begging," Cass said, folding her arms.

"Hold on Cass. We can all fall on hard times." Sandy said, reaching into her handbag. "What do you need money for, Anton?"

He looked up at the mention of his name. "You're the book lady. I need money because nobody'll gimme a job."

Sandy's cheeks flushed with guilt. "I'm sorry I couldn't help with that. Here, take this."

He held out his hand and she placed a £10 note in his palm. His mouth cracked into a smile. "Thanks, lady."

He moved on to other tables.

"You know him?" Coral asked, her nose wrinkled with disapproval.

"He came in the shop yesterday asking for work," Sandy said.

"I hope you said no," Cass said.

"Yeah, I did," Sandy said, although she wondered if she had made the right decision. Her shop was busier than ever and he needed a helping hand. Her £10 wouldn't go far for a man who lacked even the basics.

"He's staying at the Manor," Olivia said, her contribution to the conversation surprising the others.

"How do you know?" Cass asked, and it surprised Sandy

how she had developed a protective, maternal gene towards her younger sister.

Anton walked past their table again and left the pub, without acknowledging them.

"Question One!" Tom called into the microphone. He stood behind the bar, eyeing each participating table in turn. Sandy tried not to watch him too closely.

"It'll probably be, what colour are Sandy's eyes?" Cass said, descending into so much laughter they missed the real first question.

Just then there was a flurry of noise from outside.

A loud bang, a car accelerating, and then the bang of the front door being slammed open.

"Help me!" Came the distinctive voice of village eccentric and Sandy's landlord, Ignatius Potter. "You must help me! Come quickly - there's been a murder!"

3

*S*andy wore her thickest black tights, a black dress and ballet pumps the next day. Her dark outfit was a subtle way of her marking respect for the man who had been murdered. She arrived early at the cafe and found Bernice already in the kitchen, the scent of lavender rich in the room.

"Oh, Sandy," Bernice said, leaving the mixing bowl she had been working on and catching Sandy in a rare embrace. Bernice was a wonderful friend and employee, and a brilliant baker, but she was practical rather than affectionate.

"You've heard?" Sandy asked.

"I saw the news. I can't believe it's happened again." Bernice said. The recent murder of Reginald Halfman had shocked the peaceful village to its core, but with Sandy solving that case, Waterfell Tweed had never expected another murder to occur.

"I was at the pub," Sandy admitted as Bernice returned to the mixing bowl. Sprigs of lavender were visible in the cake mix, and Bernice grated lemon zest into the mixture.

"Ignatius Potter called out for help and everyone traipsed outside. It was awful."

"Ignatius Potter?" Bernice asked, tucking a strand of hair behind her ear.

"He found the poor victim, but it was too late," Sandy said as she put her own apron on. It would be an especially busy day in the cafe, as locals would use the chance for a slice of cake as an excuse to gossip about the murder.

"Do you know who the victim was? The news just said it was a homeless man."

Sandy's face blanched. "His name was Anton Carmichael."

"You knew him?" Bernice asked, her eyes appearing to water again.

"I met him once. He came in here asking for a job, and I said no." Sandy said, her voice breaking.

"Oh Sandy, don't feel bad," Bernice said.

Sandy shook her head, taking a moment to prevent the tears. "He needed help and I turned him away. I'm not proud of myself."

"But..."

"I'd rather not talk about it anymore, sorry Bernice," Sandy said as she grabbed self-raising flour, clear honey, unsalted butter and dark muscovado sugar. She placed those on the counter across from Bernice and went to the fridge for some eggs.

She hadn't ever made a honey cake for the cafe before, and didn't know what had made her think of it then. It was the cake her mum always made when she and her sister Coral were young. 'Honey for my honey' she would say as she mixed the butter, honey, and sugar in a warm pan.

When the honey mixture had cooked she set it to one side to cool and turned to sifting her flour, then added the honey mixture, beating to create a smooth batter. She added the batter to the cake tin and placed the mixture in the oven.

The act of making the cake brought memories of her mum flooding back to her. The memories were surprising in their mundanity. One memory, in particular, seemed stuck on a loop for her; her returning home from school to find her mum in the kitchen, bent down and peering through the glass of the oven door. Her hair was still the nicest Sandy had ever seen on anyone; dark brown, belly button long and incredibly glossy. That day, her mum had heard Sandy walk in the front door and turned to her with the most natural, heartwarming smile.

Sandy would love to see someone that pleased to see her now.

She sighed, her thoughts heavy with loss and regret, and left Bernice alone in the kitchen while she flicked on all of the shop lights and checked that the books were in order. Crumbs on the carpet suggested that someone had taken one of yesterday's scones upstairs, despite there being no seating up there. Sandy smiled to herself and did a full round with the old hoover, then returned downstairs and opened the door. It was early, not yet opening time, but it seemed silly to keep the door locked when she was in and ready for customers.

The door was pushed open almost immediately and Sandy felt a rush of cold air come inside, along with her neighbour Elaine Peters.

"Thank goodness you're open," Elaine said, as she pulled off her gloves and hat and took a seat by the window. "I couldn't sleep last night, had to get out."

"You could have come and knocked me up," Sandy said, although she knew Elaine would never do such a thing.

Elaine had made her way through being widowed without ever asking for help.

"That's sweet, thanks, Sandy. I think I..." She began, then glanced around the room and lowered her voice. "I missed Jim, to be honest. I'd got so used to being on my own at night and now I don't like it at all."

"Well, it wasn't a regular night, was it," Sandy said, trying to hide her surprise and happiness at the mention of Elaine's blossoming romance with Jim Slaughter, the local police constable.

"It wasn't. Who do you think did it?" Elaine asked.

"It seems open and shut," Sandy said. "Ignatius Potter was arrested."

"But was it him, Sandy? If you'd just ran someone over, why would you then call for help?"

Sandy shrugged. She had solved one murder recently and didn't plan on solving a second. She was quite happy to leave the police to do their job this time.

"And if it is him, what happens to your shop?" Elaine asked. Ignatius Potter was an eccentric man but he owned much of the village, including Sandy's own cafe and bookshop building. Not that you'd guess his wealth by looking at him. He was a loner and usually dressed in tatty old clothes that most charity shops would refuse if offered.

"I don't know." Sandy admitted. She'd like to have said the thought hadn't crossed her mind, but it had. Buildings didn't come up for sale or rent often in Waterfell Tweed, and Sandy didn't like the possibility of her business having to move out of the village.

"Well, we'll find out more soon I guess. Who knows why a young man might be homeless, what kind of trouble or enemies he's trying to get away from."

Elaine was a kind person and her comment was not meant with malice, but it troubled Sandy.

"He could just have fallen on hard times," Sandy said, defending the man who she had failed to help when he needed it. "He came in here once, he was looking at a beautiful poetry book."

"Poor lad," Elaine said as she picked up the menu from the table. "Can I get a vegetarian breakfast, please, and a mug of coffee?"

"Of course," Sandy said, pleased to get away from the conversation and busy herself with work. Elaine was the only vegetarian in the village to Sandy's knowledge, and she made sure she always had frozen vegetarian sausages in the freezer for her.

"Something smells lovely, by the way." Elaine called.

"Honey for my honey." Sandy said with a smile.

The door burst open then and a small Indian woman walked in, bundled up in a coat larger than herself.

"Morning Pritti," Sandy said, glancing up from the counter where she was making fresh coffee for Elaine.

"Good morning. Cup of hot chocolate please." She said, taking a seat at the table next to Elaine. People's seating habits fascinated Sandy. People open to talking but who didn't know the other visitors well would usually sit at the next table and strike up a conversation, while the people who did not want to speak would sit as far away from other people as they could. It was very rare that a person would join the table of someone else unless they'd planned to meet.

"How are you, Pritti? Are you getting by ok?" Elaine asked.

"Oh yes," Pritti said, appearing even smaller as she took off the large padded coat. She was a beautiful woman with perfect posture. Her posture had been the first thing Sandy had ever noticed about her. "I'm keeping very busy. Nice to have a break."

Pritti had been the housekeeper at Waterfell Manor until Benedict and Penelope Harlow had left to visit their son Sebastian.

"When will they be back?" Elaine asked. The Harlows were missed by the whole village.

Pritti shrugged. "They don't answer to me."

"Oh no, no, of course not. Please send our regards if you're speaking to them."

"I am of course speaking to them," Pritti said. Despite living in Waterfell Tweed for as long as Sandy could remember, Pritti still carried a thick Indian accent. It was rhythmic, like a song. Sandy could listen to her speak all day long.

"Did you hear about last night?" Elaine asked as Sandy placed the drinks in front of her and Pritti.

"Last night? The quiz?"

"Oh no, not the quiz. Someone was killed, Pritti." Elaine said.

"Awful business. What are the homeless doing here, anyway?" Dorie Slaughter asked, bursting into the cafe and taking a seat at the table in front of Elaine's. "Morning ladies. Full English please Sandy and a mug of tea."

"Coming right up," Sandy said and passed the food order into the kitchen for Bernice to prepare. She set to work making the tea.

"I can't believe you didn't know," Elaine said.

Pritti shrugged. "It sounds not important. Who can miss a homeless man?"

"My question is, actually I've got a lot of questions, but my question is they'd better let my Jim handle this case," Dorie said, not realising that her sentence didn't even include a question. Her son, Jim, had been removed from the last murder investigation when city police took over the case.

Sandy rolled her eyes and walked into the kitchen.

"And so it begins, eh?" Bernice asked, looking up from the two frying pans she was juggling, one containing onions, mushrooms and vegetarian sausages and the other filled with eggs, bacon, sausages, mushrooms, and onions. "I'm better off out of it in here."

"It's strange." Sandy said. "People seem to think that because Anton was homeless, his death doesn't matter."

"Well, the police won't think that. Murder is murder."

"How do they know it's murder?" Sandy asked out loud. She thought back to Ignatius Potter's cry for help the night before. "Couldn't it have been an accident?"

"No signs of braking." Sandy's sister Coral said, appearing in the kitchen doorway. She pulled off her own woollen coat and blanket scarf and pulled on her apron. "And evidence suggests the car actually accelerated, which shows intent."

4

_I_t had been a long morning, as Sandy had expected it would be. She had done her best to remain in the kitchen or upstairs hiding in the books, but she couldn't escape all of the gossip about the murder. Many of the villagers had appeared in the shop to share their theory or, more often, share random pieces of information that didn't seem to have any relevance to what had happened.

The joys of small village life!

"He's being interviewed." A voice called across the cafe. Conversations that morning had been loud and for the benefit of the whole cafe. Sandy had the start of a migraine coming on. She looked up to see Dorie Slaughter holding court, holding up her mobile phone to show a photograph of the front door of the police station as if that solved everything.

"Nice phone," Sandy said, attempting to change conversation as she made a drinks order.

"Jim and E-... Jim bought it for me." Dorie said with pride. She didn't want to think of her son being fond of a woman other than herself. Sandy smiled to herself.

"How do you know?" Poppy Sanders asked as she tucked into a sandwich on her lunch break from school, where she was a primary teacher.

"It says here. Man questioned in relation to the death of an unnamed homeless man. Ignatius Aurelius Potter, aged 57, blah blah blah… that'll be him, won't it?"

"I don't think there's another Ignatius Aurelius Potter in the village. Is he really only 57?" Coral deadpanned as she carried a single dirty plate into the kitchen.

"No, me either. Well, that's him then." Dorie said, unaware of Coral's sarcasm. "Case closed."

"An interview isn't case closed," Sandy said, thinking back to her own interview in relation to Reginald Halfman's murder. "And the man had a name, he needs to be named."

"Maybe he was in witness protection," Dorie said.

"What?" Coral asked, returning from the kitchen.

"That would explain why they won't name him. And, it would mean he'd have enemies wanting him dead."

"I don't think witness protection means you become homeless," Sandy said.

"Guys, they have the right person in an interview already. Ignatius Potter was right there, he thought getting help would make him look innocent. Or maybe he regretted it and did want to help the poor man." Coral said, placing a fresh mug of tea in front of Dorie.

"He's always been a strange one."

"Very strange."

"I've always liked him," Poppy said as she wiped her mouth with a napkin. "He's a little odd, but he makes a point of waving to the children when he walks by at playtime."

"That's weird," Coral said.

"No, it isn't Coral. The children love to wave to anyone passing - it's the people who refuse to wave back to them who are weird, in my book." Poppy said as she stood up and put her winter clothes back on. "Thanks for a lovely lunch, Sandy."

"Thanks, Poppy. See you soon." Sandy said.

"What's got into her?" Coral asked after Poppy had left and the door had closed behind her.

"She's too soft, that one," Dorie said. "Won't see the bad in anyone. Even that drunk of a husband."

Sandy sighed and walked through the cafe and up the stairs. The upper floor, where most of the books were, was always quieter than the cafe, and it had become something of a sanctuary for Sandy. She would never want to wish custom away, as she much preferred the shop being busy and the takings being high enough to pay the bills with ease, but she was an introvert at heart and sometimes she had to break away and find a quiet space.

"Ah, good afternoon Sandy." A rich voice greeted her as she poked her head around one of the aisles of bookcases.

"Good afternoon, Rob," Sandy said, pleased to see the vicar. Rob Fields was a man who exuded peace and tranquility. His presence was enough to make Sandy consider finding God.

"Am I in your way?" He asked, gesturing to the bookcase in front of him. To Sandy's surprise, he was standing by the painting section.

"Not at all, please carry on. I didn't realise you were an artist?"

Rob let out a quiet laugh and blushed. "I'd hardly say that. I'm dabbling with watercolours and I need guidance!"

"I bet you're doing brilliantly," Sandy said, and she meant it. He was such an understated man, she expected that he could be shortlisted for a fine art award and would downplay his skill as beginner's luck.

"And how are you doing?" Rob asked. It was a casual question but his tone and profession gave it a deeper, more concerned air.

Sandy took a deep breath and paused for a moment, deciding to answer the vicar honestly instead of giving the usual pleasantry she would to anyone else who asked how she was. "I'm feeling guilty, actually."

"Ah, guilt. The most troubling emotion. Do you want to share?" He offered.

"The man who was killed last night, he asked me for a job recently and I said no."

"And you wish you had said yes?"

"Well, I, I guess so."

"Sandy, we cannot save everyone," Rob said, still looking at the books rather than her. His lack of eye contact made her feel as if she was in confession, something she had never done.

"I could have done more," Sandy whispered. "That's where the guilt comes from. I could have done more."

"Then do more," Rob said, finally glancing at her.

"What? He's dead now?"

"There are plenty more in his situation. If you wish you had done more then, do more now." Rob said as he selected three books from the shelf. He gave Sandy a smile, squeezed her arm, and then walked away.

Sandy stood in the same spot for some time, lost in her thoughts. The vicar was right. There were plenty of other people in need, and she could help some of them even if she hadn't helped Anton.

She returned downstairs to the bustling cafe, which had grown even busier while she had been upstairs. A quick glance out of the window confirmed the reason - heavy rain was falling outside. Everyone was darting inside for shelter.

The scene made Sandy contemplate the reality of being homeless, of seeking shelter wherever possible in a world that rarely wanted to help.

"I'm going to head out for a bit." She called to Bernice and Coral as she grabbed her bright yellow mac.

"In this weather? Is everything ok?" Coral asked.

"I'm fine," Sandy said. "Can you wrap me up some loaves of bread and that joint of beef we haven't sliced yet?"

Coral eyed her sister but asked no more questions, disappearing into the kitchen.

Bernice appeared a few moments later, carrying a tray filled to the brim with bread and beef. Sandy spotted a cake box in there. "Here you go, it'd have taken Coral all day bringing this load out one slice of bread at a time."

Sandy laughed at the joke. Her sister was great with customers but useless with the more hands-on elements of working in a cafe. Luckily, Bernice was happy to remain behind the scenes doing all of that side of the job.

She loaded the tray into the boot of her old Land Rover and then got in the driver's seat, already soaked through from the brief time in the rain. She had been tempted to delay this errand when she saw the rain falling, but she realised quickly that she was lucky to have a choice and a warm building to stay in. Not everyone was that lucky.

Turning up the temperamental heating in her old car she began the short drive across the village square and past the church to the grand entrance for Waterfell Manor. The Manor house had been home to the aristocratic Harlow family for centuries, and most of the homes in the village had been built for servants of the Manor and their families.

She drove up the winding path, her windscreen wipers

flicking from side to side as quickly as they could to remove the rain. Finally, she reached the gravel drive of the Manor and parked in front of the building.

She didn't know what she had been expecting but it hadn't been what she saw. The Manor looked as it always had. The way people had spoken about the squatters in the Manor house, she had expected to see the building crumbling or burnt to the ground.

She sat in the car for a few minutes with the engine off, just watching. There was nobody around at all. All of the curtains were closed and Sandy guessed that would be to warm the cavernous building, as the heating would have been switched off before the Harlows left weeks earlier.

She was about to summon the courage to step out of the car when a tap came to the passenger window.

Sandy jumped and reached for the knob to lock the door, then saw the young man standing by her door. He looked around 16 years old and was dressed in jeans and a hoodie.

"Are you ok?" He called through the glass. "Are you lost?"

Sandy wound the window down and the rain poured in, reaching across to her side of the car and hitting her face and chest. "I'm from the village, I heard that people were living in here."

"What's it to you, lady?" The boy asked. "Are you police?"

"No!" Sandy cried. She had expected a warm welcome, but she saw now how suspicious it must appear for her to have arrived the day after one of their own was killed. "I want to help."

"Help how?"

"I run the cafe in the village, I've brought food."

"Yeah?" The boy asked, attempting to play it cool. His face betrayed him and a small smile escaped from his serious expression.

"There's not lots, it was a spur of the moment idea, but I can bring more."

"Let's see then." The boy asked as he moved to the back of the vehicle. He peered through the boot window at the tray of food and grinned.

Sandy wound the window back up and jumped out of the car, putting her hood up before she even climbed out. "It's bread and beef, and I think there's a cake too."

"Beef?" The boy asked, and Sandy pointed to the slab of meat in its clear packing. "A whole joint? Fair play!"

"Can you carry it in?" Sandy asked, not keen to enter the Manor herself unaccompanied.

"Yeah, lady, leave it to me." The boy said. Sandy wondered if he would share it or keep it for himself. She had no idea if squatters had a code of conduct or if it was each person for themselves.

"Before I go..." Sandy said as the boy walked away with the tray of food. "Would it help if I brought more?"

"It'd be more of a help than anyone else is giving." The boy called, then continued walking. Sandy opened her front door and watched him approach the side of the Manor.

"Hey!" He called when he was virtually out of sight. "Thanks, lady. Thanks a lot."

Sandy grinned and climbed back into her car, hoping the boy and whoever else he was with had access to part of the Manor that would keep them warm and dry. She couldn't help thinking that if the Harlow family knew they were in there, they would want them to be looked after.

"Well, well, well." A voice came from behind Sandy as

she was about to close her front door. She turned to see a familiar face climbing out of his own car. "Fancy seeing you here."

Sandy took a gulp then gave her best smile. "DC Sullivan, what a small world."

$\mathcal{T}$he pain was immense.

Definitely worse than the time before.

"You're making such a fuss, honestly I've never heard anything like it." Cass scolded as she tore the waxing strip from Sandy's eyebrow.

"It hurts, Cass! I don't know why I came back again." Sandy whimpered.

"Because you didn't want to look like a Yeti, that's why!" Cass teased. "I've seen gorillas less hairy."

"Hey!" Sandy exclaimed as Cass applied a layer of hot wax to the skin underneath her nose. "Careful with that stuff!"

"I didn't spill it, hold still."

"What are you doing now?"

"Getting rid of this moustache." Cass said, tearing the wax from above Sandy's upper lip.

"Argh!" Sandy screamed, jumping up from the treatment bed. "Enough!"

"Ok, ok, I've done anyway. We'll do your legs next time." Cass said as she washed her hands. "That'll be £8 please."

"I can't believe you're allowed to charge to torture people," Sandy said, holding out a crisp £10 note. "Keep the change in exchange for never seeing me in here again."

"Don't be daft," Cass said, forcing a £2 coin in her hand. "You'll be back."

"You're like a James Bond villain Cass, honestly." Sandy said, moving across to the waiting area and plopping herself down on a chair. "Got time for a coffee?"

Cass looked at the clock on the wall. "Go on then, I've got twenty minutes."

"How's Olivia doing?" Sandy asked. Olivia was Cass' 15-year-old step-sister who had recently moved in with Cass after running away from her foster carers.

Cass rolled her eyes. "I thought I was still young before Olivia was here. Now I feel ancient. There's a new teenage drama every week. You'd imagine that Olivia wouldn't have time for things like that after everything she's been through."

"Maybe she's enjoying the chance to be a regular kid?" Sandy suggested.

"Yeah... She's got a boyfriend now, that's the latest."

"A boyfriend?" Sandy asked as Cass placed a cup of weak kettle coffee in front of them both.

"I haven't met him, know nothing about him, and she thinks I'm unreasonable to want to know about him. Fifteen seems so young to have a boyfriend."

"Excuse me?" Sandy said, almost spitting her coffee out. "I remember you and Tommy Fisher being serious when you were fifteen."

"Tommy Fisher!" Cass exclaimed. "There's a blast from the past. He broke my heart on my 16th birthday."

"That's how I know you were all loved up when you were Olivia's age. I remember drying your tears."

"He was so lovely when he wasn't being a moron." Cass said,. "I wonder what happened to him."

"His family left the village, didn't they?"

"I think so. I might ask my mum, bet she'll remember. You're right though, I look at Olivia now and think she's a child but when I was her age I knew I was a grown up. Geeze, do you remember the things we wore then?"

Sandy laughed. "I remember the things you made me wear!"

"There was that day that we went out in jeans, do you remember, and we snuck into the shed on my garden and changed into the tiniest little skirts."

"Matching skirts - yours was white and mine was a red wine colour."

"That's it! We walked around thinking we looked amazing."

"And then we saw those college boys from out of town and you said they would whistle at us and they..."

"...threw blackberries at us instead! Our skirts were ruined!" They both finished the story in unison before descending into laughter. The memory was so fresh in Sandy's mind. She'd never worn a skirt that short again in her life.

"The things we did." Cass said, smiling at the memory.

"We've been through a lot, hey." Sandy agreed.

Cass shook her head. "It probably won't hurt if I remember some of these things when I talk to Olivia. She seems smitten with this boy."

"She'll get that from you, falling in love hard." Sandy teased.

"That's true. And she might grow up like us and be stuck single so she should enjoy it while she can." Cass joked.

"Right, I'm off. Thanks for the drink. Not thanks for the pain." Sandy said as she stood up. She reached over and gave Cass a kiss on the side of her cheek, already knowing she would be back four weeks later for another eyebrow wax. She dreaded to think what else Cass might try to pour hot wax on that time.

**

The cafe was busy again when Sandy returned.

Coral was working on the till, flashing her winning smile at Jim Slaughter, who was placing an order at the counter.

"Oh, Jim, hello," Sandy said. "I ran into our friend DC Sullivan yesterday."

Jim turned to her and his expression revealed that the Detective Constable's return from the city was news to him. "He's back?"

"Sorry, I thought you'd have known."

"I can't believe they've done this again. I interviewed Mr. Potter, I thought I'd be working the case this time."

"Sorry, Jim," Sandy said. "Hopefully DC Sullivan will take your ideas on board more this time."

"There's no need for ideas and no need for city police," Jim whined. He sounded like a sulking toddler.

Sandy looked at Coral.

"Well sit down Jim, it sounds like you need some cake to go with that cappuccino. Shall we say lemon drizzle or chocolate fudge?"

Jim gave a cheeky smile. "Let's say a slice of each."

"I like your style. I'll bring it right over." Coral said as Jim turned to look for an empty table. He walked away and Coral eyed her sister. "DC Sullivan back in town? That has to mean the case isn't as open and shut as we thought."

"To be honest, I think city have heard the word murder and stuck their nose in. And I don't want to know anything else. I'm not being dragged into it this time."

"Ok!" Coral said, holding her hands up in defence.

"Morning, Auntie Sandy." A voice came from the counter. There was only one person who called her that, and it was such a new name it made her jump each time.

She turned to see Olivia, still in her school uniform, and holding hands with the boy who Sandy had seen at the Manor the day before.

"Olivia, what are you doing here? And hello again to your... friend." Sandy said.

"This is Derrick, he's my boyfriend," Olivia said with pride. Sandy's heart raced at the obvious display of first love.

"Hello, Derrick," Sandy said, giving the boy a smile.

"Hello again, lady."

"You two know each other?" Olivia asked, in the jealous way that teenage girls reserved for any aspect of their crush's life that they weren't aware of.

"We met yesterday. Is it your lunch break?" Sandy asked.

"Free period. Derrick came and met me for a walk."

"She was talking about her big sister and auntie a lot so I suggested I meet them," Derrick said, his cheeks flushing as he spoke. "Cassie is a bit mad, isn't she?"

"She sure is." Sandy agreed, noting how he used Olivia's nickname for her big sister. "She's wonderful, though. Do you want some food?"

"We don't have much time." Derrick blurted. "I don't want you back late for school."

"Sit yourselves down and I'll make something on the house, then I can drive you back."

The two lovebirds beamed at each other and found the most secluded table they could. Sandy watched them and smiled, then grabbed two jacket potatoes from the oven and placed each one on a plate, slicing the potatoes down the middle and adding butter and cheese and a hearty side salad. She lay two slices of ham on each plate, which she wouldn't usually do.

"Here you go." She said, placing the food in front of the teenagers. She noted that they were still holding hands.

"Thanks, auntie Sandy," Olivia said.

"Thanks, lady," Derrick said.

She walked away and left them to eat, and when they stood up ten minutes later she pulled on her yellow rain mac. "I'm driving Olivia back to school, be back in a few."

Olivia sat in the front passenger seat at Derrick's insistence, and they made the drive to school while chatting.

"Here we are," Sandy said as she pulled up outside the school. Teenagers were milling around making their way back on the school grounds, which told her they had timed it ok and not missed the bell.

"I'm going to walk Olivia in, thanks for the lift Sandy," Derrick said.

"I'll wait for you and take you where you need to go," Sandy said, and Derrick nodded.

Olivia gave her a kiss on the cheek and Sandy watched them walk away hand in hand. The sight made her heart glad.

Derrick was back in sight a few seconds later, walking back towards the car. He sat in the passenger seat and waited for Sandy to begin the conversation.

"Where are you headed?" She asked, feeling like a taxi driver.

"I have nowhere to go," Derrick admitted. "I'll probably

just hang around at the Manor until school finishes, then I'll walk back down to walk Olivia home."

"That's very gentlemanly," Sandy said.

Derrick shrugged. "My dad always said to treat a girl like a princess."

"Is your dad... is he at the Manor?"

"Nah. He died."

"I'm so sorry," Sandy said, her eyes filling with tears.

"Mum lost the house after that. Council put her up but it's a tiny place and she's got the young uns, no room for me."

"She kicked you out?"

"Nah! No way... I did her a favour and left. There's no jobs so I were another mouth to feed and the food already weren't feeding them. I'm big enough to look after myself."

"How old are you, Derrick?"

"Seventeen." He mumbled. "Olivia knows. And I know she's underage, don't worry."

"I'm not worried," Sandy said, struck by his honesty. "Does Olivia know... everything?"

"Nah, she thinks I live out of town. Which I do... I did. It's embarrassing, I don't want her to think I'm some waster. All I need is a chance, I've been applying for jobs and when I get some money coming in I can go back home."

"Derrick, are you any good at washing pots?"

He laughed. "Every other day for sixteen years, well, bit less, that was my job."

"Come and work for me." Sandy offered.

"Ya kidding?"

"It's minimum wage and I can't promise how many hours it would be every week, but we're definitely busy enough now to need an extra pair of hands."

"I don't want no charity," Derrick said. "Who am I

kidding? I need any help I can get. Thanks, lady, if you've got pots I can wash them."

Sandy grinned. "Come on then, you said you have no other plans, fancy your first shift?"

"Sounds good," Derrick said as they pulled up outside Books and Bakes. "Can I ring my mum and tell her the news?"

"Of course you can," Sandy said, then realised he meant with her phone. "Here, you make your call and come on in when you're done."

She handed him her phone and as she was climbing out of the car, heard the start of his conversation.

"Mum, it's me. I know, I know, don't cry... I've got good news..."

6

*D*errick was a machine at pot washing.

His years of every-other-night training that his dad had insisted upon had paid off and it was quickly evident that he would need other jobs to fill his time. Thankfully, with so many customers to serve, there was plenty for him to do.

"How are you at changing lightbulbs?" Bernice asked him towards the end of his second day of work.

"Yeah, I can do that," Derrick said and followed her into the men's toilets where a customer had reported the light wasn't working. Bernice left him to it and returned to the counter.

"He's nice." She said. From practical Bernice, the comment was high praise.

"I like him," Coral said, but she was easier to win over. As long as a person acted interested in, and impressed by, her former journalist career, Coral would like them.

"I'm going to go to the Manor again later, can we sort out some more bread and meat? If there's any jackets left, I'll take those too." Sandy said. She had decided that if she gave

Derrick a lift back to the Manor, he could take the food in for her.

"I could rustle up some more cake too." Bernice offered.

"Great idea."

The door opened then, the bell announcing another customer. Poppy Sanders walked in, concentrating on a telephone conversation she was in the middle of.

"Just come and meet me now, and calm down." She said, taking a seat at the only free table, which was closest to the counter. She ended the call and took a deep breath.

"You look like you need cake," Coral said, whizzing across to her with her notepad.

A few minutes later, the door burst open and Poppy's husband, Gus, stormed in. His face was bright red and his hands were shaking. "I've had it!"

"Just sit down, Gus," Poppy ordered, and the man did as his wife told him.

"I'm not gonna keep putting up with this," Gus said as he sat down and tossed the menu on the floor. Coral raised an eyebrow.

'We'll get a coffee each, no food." Poppy told Coral, who nodded and walked away.

"What's got into him?" Coral whispered to Sandy as she returned to the counter. The two sisters turned their backs on the cafe to face the large coffee machine.

"I don't know," Sandy said. Gus Sanders was known as a hothead. He was a drinker and had occasionally been accompanied out of The Tweed after one too many. But he was also a respected businessman; he'd run the butchers in the village square since taking it over from his father. That was how businesses worked in Waterfell Tweed, one brave person would begin one and pass it down to their children who would pass it down to their children. The thought made Sandy wonder who would take over Books and Bakes when the time came.

"If I catch them at it, they'll be sorry," Gus shouted.

"Gus, calm down. Please." Poppy urged.

"It's time to take this into my own hands!" He said as he pushed his chair back and stood up, then stormed out of the cafe.

The rest of the customers descended into quiet gossip about his outburst, while Poppy buried her head in her hands.

"Coffee and cake," Coral said as she placed a cup of coffee and a slice of rich chocolate fudge cake in front of Poppy.

"I said no food, the cake must be for someone else." Poppy said, pushing it away.

"Looks like you need it," Coral said. "What's wrong with Gus?"

"Oh, he blows up and then he's fine again, it will blow over. He's found more graffiti at the shop." Poppy explained.

"I thought that had stopped?" Coral asked.

"It stops and starts. The police can't seem to find out who's doing it. We put CCTV up on the front so now they do the side or the back instead. Whoever it is, they're smart."

"And vegetarian." Dorie Slaughter called. She was sitting at the next table.

"Vegetarian?"

"All the graffiti is about animal rights," Poppy said as she dug a fork into the slab of chocolate cake.

"Weird," Coral said. "There aren't any vegetarians around here..."

"There's Elaine Peters," Poppy said, with a laugh. "I can't imagine her with a can of spray paint."

"It's not Elaine Peters." Dorie Slaughter said. Elaine was dating her son, Jim. "She's practically family."

"Are things going that well?" Sandy asked.

"I always told him he needed a homely woman, none of those glamorous ones he was after. It's alright having one whose nice to look at, but can she clean? That's what I want to know."

Coral shook her head and laughed.

"Elaine keeps a beautiful home," Dorie admitted. "And that's my point. The women who keep a beautiful painted face can't be keeping a home too. You can't have both."

Sandy rolled her eyes. Dorie's opinions were strong, unfounded and changed day by day.

"Pritti Sharma had both." Poppy said. "She kept the Manor and she's a lovely looking woman."

"That's different." Dorie dismissed. "She doesn't wear make-up, she was born nice looking. She's just lucky."

"Not lucky now," Coral said. "She must drive herself mad with nothing to do with her time."

"She's still getting paid, I reckon," Dorie said and a few other customers murmured their agreement. The Harlows wouldn't disappear across the world and leave their staff without income. "She should have moved in, that'd have stopped the squatters."

"She's got a family." Poppy said. "She can't move out and leave her own children."

"Imagine it though, watching your pride and glory be taken over by those people."

"Can we talk about something else?" Sandy asked, wanting to change the subject before Derrick finished his repair work in the toilet.

"I'd best be going anyway," Dorie said as she slurped the last of her tea. The old woman filled most of her days in the cafe, and in the bad months, her custom had helped Sandy pay vital bills. She liked to gossip, but she was harmless and loyal to Books and Bakes.

"Night, Dorie," Sandy called as she walked out.

The rest of the customers seemed to look at their watches and realise it was almost closing time, and within a few minutes, most of the tables became empty.

"Thanks for listening to me moan," Poppy said as she stood and put her own winter clothes back on.

"Anytime," Sandy said with a smile. "Let us know if we can do anything to help Gus."

Poppy nodded and left.

Derrick, Bernice, and Coral were all in the kitchen washing the last pots and tidying everything away, when Sandy walked over to lock the front door. She jumped when she saw a man's face in the glass looking at her.

"Mr. Potter!" She cried, opening the door for her landlord. "You made me jump."

"Thought you'd seen a ghost, did you?" He asked. He walked with a stick and gave off a musty smell. A single pea sat in the middle of his white beard.

"No, not at all. Are you ok?" Sandy asked. She rarely saw Ignatius Potter, despite him having been her landlord since she first moved into the shop building. He preferred to communicate with her by hand-scrawled letters delivered through the letterbox by hand overnight, and always with her name spelled wrong.

"Yes, yes. I came to find Dorothy."

"Dorothy?" Sandy asked, used to the shortened version of her best customer's name. "Oh, Dorie? You've just missed her."

"Typical. Did she say where she was going?"

"No, she didn't. Can I pass on a message?"

"I thought we were meeting here. I must have the details wrong." He said, as a gust of wind almost knocked him off his feet. "Can you give me a lift home?"

"Don't you have your car?" Sandy asked, confused by the exchange. She couldn't imagine why Ignatius Potter would imagine he had plans with Dorie Slaughter.

"The police have it. Evidence! I don't know what they think they'll find."

"I'd imagine they'll look for signs of whether it hit Anton."

"Well, of course it didn't. I told them that. I was the one who found him and fetched help, and I missed my chess club."

"Chess club?"

"Yes, chess club. You do know what chess is, don't you?" He asked, and his breathing became laboured as he stood before Sandy.

"Come on in, Mr. Potter. We can sort out getting you home. Come and have a seat." Sandy said, leading him inside to the nearest chair. She locked the door behind them.

"So, this is what you've done with the space, then?" He asked, looking around the cafe and across to the small book area at the far end of the shop. "What is it, cakes and books?"

"That's it," Sandy said, trying not to laugh at the idea that her landlord had no idea what she had been doing in a shop called Books and Bakes.

"People like this kind of thing, don't they? Paying through the nose for things they can get for free!"

"Well... some people like to relax with a coffee and a book." Sandy said.

"A library and a kettle, that's all people need. They can't

spend their money quick enough." Ignatius continued, then a fit of coughing took over.

"Guys," Sandy said, poking her head in the kitchen doorway. "Ignatius Potter has just turned up. I don't think he's well, I'm going to drive him home."

"I'll sort Derrick and the food for the Manor." Bernice offered, and Sandy gave her a grateful smile.

"See you all tomorrow." She said. "Come on, Mr. Potter, let's get you home."

Sandy had never been to Ignatius Potter's home before and didn't even know where it was. She imagined it to be as battered and eccentric as he was.

"Keep going down this road." He instructed from the passenger seat.

"What will you do about Dor... Dorothy? What were you meeting her for?" Sandy asked, unable to resist knowing more.

"It's not a big deal. She left her scarf when I saw her last, that's all." He explained, pulling a fancy silk scarf from the inside of his jacket. It definitely belonged to Dorie; Sandy had seen her wear it many times.

"She comes in the cafe most days, I can pass it back to her."

"Ah, now that would be useful. I do hate the trek into the village." He said, reaching over to put the scarf on the back seat. "Keep going, and it's the second left coming up."

There were fields on either side of the road and no buildings in sight, which didn't surprise Sandy. She could picture Ignatius Potter living in an isolated building where he could avoid people.

"Pass a message on to Dorothy for me?"

"Of course."

"Tell her the gardening club isn't what it used to be but

she'd enjoy the book club perhaps. They try to get me to join but I'll stick with chess." Ignatius said, as they reached the end of the small road that had been the second turning he had instructed her to take.

A large building stood before then, and the sign read *The Foxglove: Waterfell Tweed Assisted Living Community.*

7

*P*oppy Sanders arrived for the children's book time early, as usual. She brought her teaching efficiency to the group, each week selecting a mixture of books to read and songs to sing. She knew how long the group would last and what the learning objectives would be. It was a popular free group that most of the village locals who had children attended.

"Fancy a coffee?" Sandy asked as Poppy walked in armed with a large box.

"No, I've got stage fright, I'd rather get myself focused."

"Stage fright? What are you planning?"

"We're going to sing." Poppy said, and her cheeks flushed.

"You've sung before, haven't you?" Sandy asked.

"No, I've avoided songs because I can't sing. Honestly, Sandy, my singing voice is like a cat being strangled - worse than that even! But the children have been requesting a song. So, I'm going to give it a whirl."

"You'll be brilliant," Sandy reassured, thinking again how lucky she was to have someone volunteer their time.

The group was a highlight of the week for the children of the sleepy village, and as a teacher Poppy was committed to doing all she could to help the village children, but the group also meant that Sunday mornings were incredibly busy for Books and Bakes as parents strolled through the book aisles and bought coffee and cake to pass the time.

She watched Poppy walk over to the small book area at the far end of the downstairs, and returned to her thoughts. She could not forget about her strange interaction with Ignatius Potter since the night before.

"Penny for them?" Coral asked, emerging from the kitchen with beans on toast for a customer. She placed the food in front of the stranger and returned to Sandy's side.

"How much do you know about Ignatius Potter?" Sandy asked her sister.

"About as much as anyone does, he's like an international man of mystery to say how much of the village he owns."

"Have you ever been to his house or anything?"

"No, of course not. What's it like?"

Sandy looked around the cafe. "This stays between us, okay? He doesn't live in a house. He lives in a care home."

"A care home?" Coral repeated, her mouth open wide in surprise.

"Well, an assisted living community. And, I think Dorie wants to move in it too."

"Dorie Slaughter?" Coral asked. "Why would she want to leave the village?"

"I've been thinking about that. Think about how much time she spends in here, she's pretty much here every day, and that's got to be because she's lonely."

"And if she lived in one of those things she'd have people around her all the time," Coral said, nodding her head. "Do you think Jim's paying her less attention now he's with Elaine?"

"Well, Elaine told me that he's been staying at hers quite a lot."

"So Dorie's going home to an empty house when she leaves here," Coral said. "How sad."

"Talk of the devil," Sandy said, noticing Dorie walking across the village square towards the shop.

"Good morning," Dorie called as she burst into the shop, bringing the cold air with her. "Full English today, please, and a mug of Earl Grey."

"Earl Grey?" Sandy asked. "That's not your normal, Dorie, mixing it up a bit?"

"Don't patronise me." The old woman barked, noting the extra friendliness in Sandy's voice. "I read a fascinating article about all the health properties of it... can't remember a blinking one of them now. Maybe memory was one of them, eh?"

Sandy laughed. "It's worth a try. Oh, Dorie, I've got your scarf... someone left it for you."

Dorie's face clouded with a memory and her skin turned white.

"Are you ok?" Sandy asked.

"No, no I'm not. Oh, my goodness." Dorie said, clasping her hand over her mouth.

"What's wrong?" Sandy asked, taking the seat next to Dorie.

"Did Mr. Potter bring this for me?"

"Oh, yes, don't worry," Sandy said, realising that Dorie must have remembered the meeting she hadn't turned up for. "He said he thought you were going to meet to get it back but he misunderstood."

"No, that's not it, I told him to hand it in here whenever

he was passing, but oh my goodness. I can't believe I didn't think."

"Didn't think what, Dorie? You're worrying me."

"He was dragged in for questioning and I was so busy being proud that my Jim was doing the interview I didn't think about anything else. Mr. Potter couldn't have run over that man - he was with me."

"He wasn't with you, Dorie, you weren't in the car when he stopped," Sandy said.

"Whoever did this, Sandy, they ran over the man and drove away. If it had been Mr. Potter, he'd have had to have run over him, drove away and made a circle to come back on himself to then stop and get help. Do you see?"

"Yes... I get that, but you weren't there Dorie."

Dorie sighed in frustration. "I was outside the police station. Mr. Potter had dropped me off there so I could check on Jim, he hadn't gone out with a coat that day and it was so cold. I hadn't even gone inside the door by the time Mr. Potter was calling for help."

"If he had done it, you'd have heard," Sandy said, with a gasp.

"Well, of course. I may be falling apart in many ways but I'd hear a man being run over. I need to go to the police." Dorie said as she jumped up from her seat. She darted out of the cafe and turned right to walk the few doors down to the police station.

**

The rest of the day continued as normal.

The children's book group was a huge success, with even the adults cheering for Poppy's singing. She was spot on about her singing talent, but everyone admired her courage.

"Such a good teacher." Pritti Sharma said. She had never attended the group when she was working at the Manor but had been a regular face for the groups since. She busied herself upstairs looking at books and occasionally buying instead of relaxing with a coffee as many other parents did.

"She's excellent." A proud Gus Sanders called. He was standing by the counter and Sandy tried to ignore the faint whiff of alcohol on his breath. It was lunchtime and there was nothing wrong with a lunchtime drink, after all.

"How are you, Gus?" Sandy asked.

To her surprise, he grinned. "I'm blooming marvellous. I've got a plan to catch the little toe-rag and his spray paint, and then I'll be even better."

"Well, be careful," Sandy said, feeling the spark of danger that she often felt Gus Sanders radiate.

He laughed.

"Are you ok for a few minutes?" Sandy asked Coral, who nodded her agreement mid-bite of a fruit scone. She had been gaining weight ever since joining the cafe because she couldn't resist the food around her. Sandy left her sister to it and pulled up a chair next to her best friend, Cass, who was eating a jacket potato and scrolling on her phone.

"Hey," Sandy said. "You ok?"

"Not really, Sand. I can't stop worrying. I know I'm being silly."

"Is this about Olivia?"

"Olivia and Derrick. You've met him, what do you think?"

Sandy pictured her newest employee, his eagerness to please and readiness to do any job she asked him to. "I really like him Cass. He's such a gentleman."

"Hmm." Cass murmured.

"Don't you think so?"

"I don't dislike him," Cass admitted. "He seems nice and he always walks Olivia home and I appreciate that, but she's so head over heels for him."

"She's a teenager, it's probably her first love. It could all fizzle out in a few weeks." Sandy said, although she didn't think that would be the case.

"I don't want her... I don't want her getting hurt." Cass whispered. "She's been through too much for that."

"Do you think that's a possibility?"

"No," Cass admitted. "She's got a good head on her shoulders, and I think he has too. It seems so much, so quick. I mean, a boy wanting to meet the family? That's heavy, isn't it?"

"I think it shows he wants to do things properly. It's old-fashioned, I like it."

"I just really don't want her to get hurt." Cass confided. "He's all she talks about."

"Cass, she's a teenager. If it fizzles out or goes wrong, we'll look after her. Come on, we survived heartbreak ourselves. You got over Tommy Fisher."

"Stop saying that name." Cass laughed. "I think if he walked back in here now I'd give him a telling off."

"So you should," Sandy said. "And imagine the telling off you can give Derrick if he messes up. Just give him the chance to prove himself, not everything has to end badly."

"Says you. How full is your love life at the moment?" Cass asked.

"Empty as you know, but that's not the point."

"Did you hear any more from Tom Nelson after he spent all quiz night eyeing you up?"

"Tom Nelson was not eyeing me up," Sandy said, but the mention of his name made her stomach flip. She remembered the way he had been looking at her, or had appeared to have been looking at her, and how good it had felt. "And I'm happy single."

"Oh come on, we're happy single unless the right man comes along. You wouldn't turn The Hunk away and neither would I!"

"Well, I'm not going to fight you for him," Sandy said.

"I've had my chance." Cass admitted.

"What? Tell me everything!"

"Oh it was years ago, a friend of his set us up for a blind date. It was awful, Sandy. He's much more your sort. We spent the whole night making awkward small talk, then I suggested I needed an early night and left. He's a lovely guy, but all he wanted to talk about was books."

"You are winding me up," Sandy said. The idea of the village's most eligible bachelor being a book lover was too much to believe.

"Nope. I swear."

"Why doesn't he ever come in the shop then, if he loves books?"

"Probably intimidated by your beauty," Cass said with a shrug as she forked the last bite of jacket potato in her mouth.

"Shut up." Sandy teased. "I'm going to leave you to your step-sister worries."

Cass smirked as Sandy left the table.

"I will buy this." Pritti Sharma said, approaching the counter with a hardback book about English country gardens.

"This looks good," Sandy said. "Are you into gardening?"

"Not for me, it's the birthday of Manor gardener." Pritti explained.

"Shall I gift-wrap it?" Sandy asked. She had set up a small counter upstairs for gift wrapping.

"No, Sanjeev will do." She said, rustling the hair of the little boy who stood by her side. "He enjoys wrapping."

"Excellent." Sandy said, addressing the child. "That's a grown-up job."

"I do it because mummy isn't home." The boy explained.

"Children." Pritti said, rolling her eyes. "So dramatic. Mummy works hard to put food on your table. Nobody else is going to."

"Bye!" Sandy called. As she watched most of the parents and children who had gathered for the reading time gather bundles of coats and shoes and socks and dummies and juice bottles and teddy bears and sodden blankets and pushchairs and shopping bags and who knows what else, she wondered what her life would have been like if she had met the right man and had a family.

She was sure that wouldn't happen for her now.

At least with the shop, she could bring happiness to the village children in some small way.

And with none of the mess or sleepless nights that having her own child would require from her.

8

*D*orie Slaughter arrived as usual for breakfast, bundled into a raincoat with a Russian fur hat standing proud on her head. Sandy withheld a laugh at the bizarre pairing of items and finished arranging the day's cakes in the glass-fronted display case.

A red velvet cake stood proud, uncut and glorious, on the highest cake stand. Around it were Sandy's lemon curd tarts, Bernice's hazelnut torte and a brand new experiment - treacle toffee sponge pudding, which had made the kitchen smell divine.

"Morning, Dorie." Sandy called. "I'll be over in a minute."

"Don't bother, you should check the kitchen. Smells like something's on fire." Dorie moaned.

"Hmm." Sandy mumbled, wrinkling her nose and taking a sniff. There was a definite hint of spice along with the sweetness of the cooked treacle, but Sandy wouldn't describe as a burnt smell. "It's the new cake, Dorie. Treacle toffee sponge pudding."

"If you say so." Dorie said. She was sitting at a table far

from the counter, her coat over the chair but the hat still standing tall on her head.

"Nice hat." Sandy said as she walked over to Dorie with her notepad. "What can I get you?"

"None of that cake, that's for sure." Dorie grumbled. "Sausage sandwich and a pot of tea."

"Ok." Sandy said, writing the order down to buy her time to build her nerve. "Dorie, can I ask you, are you okay?"

Dorie sighed. "They're all the same, aren't they?"

"Who?" Sandy asked as the doorbell rang to announce another visitor. Dorie turned to see Elaine Peters walk in, glance nervously at Dorie, and then loiter around at the counter.

"Oh well isn't that perfect timing." Dorie moaned, picking up the menu and eyeing it.

Sandy left her to it. Whatever had happened was none of her business.

"Good morning, Elaine. What can I get for you?" Sandy asked as she passed the food order back through to the kitchen for Bernice.

"Sorry, I'm late!" Coral called then, bursting through the door. "I swear I set my alarm, I don't know what happened!"

"It's fine, don't worry, we're still quiet." Sandy said, gesturing towards the cafe that was empty apart from Dorie. Elaine remained focused on looking at the till only.

"Can I get two bacon sandwiches... to go?" She whispered, her cheeks flushing red.

"Of course, coming right up." Sandy said. She passed the order back through to Bernice and asked her to hurry the food along. The tension between Dorie and Elaine could be cut with a knife.

"Aren't you speaking, then?" Dorie called out then, putting her menu back down on the table.

Elaine spun on her heels, faced Dorie and burst into the largest, most artificial smile Sandy had ever seen. "Dorie! I didn't notice you. How nice to see you!"

"What a load of rubbish." Dorie said. "Where is he?"

Elaine stood open-mouthed, blinking. "He?"

"He?! My son! Where is my son? I rang him last night and he didn't answer, and I haven't heard from him since. Has he forgot where he lives?"

Elaine's cheeks were bright red. "Oh, Dorie, I will ask him to call you if I... if I see him."

Dorie rolled her eyes. "Make sure you do. I might not be here much longer."

Sandy's ears pricked up at the last comment.

Dorie's suffocating love for her son had been a source of plenty of teasing to her face over the years, but Sandy knew that deep down it all boiled down to the fact that Dorie didn't really have anyone else. She had been widowed many years ago and had reacted to that loss by making her entire world revolve around her son.

It must be hard for her to see him enjoying the company of another woman and having less time for his mother.

"Bacon sandwiches!" Coral called, emerging from the kitchen with two brown bags, which she handed to Elaine, who gave her a grateful squeeze of her hand.

"Well, I must be off, goodbye Dorie, so nice to see you!" Elaine called as she practically ran out of the cafe.

"I don't know what my Jim sees in her." Dorie muttered.

"I thought you were pleased he'd found a, erm, homely woman?" Sandy asked as she pulled up a seat and joined Dorie at her table.

"He had a homely woman right here." Dorie said, giving a big sigh as Coral placed her breakfast order in front of her.

"He's probably a bit wrapped up in things at the

moment, with the murder too. Why don't you do some more things for yourself, Dorie?"

"Like what? What good am I?" Dorie asked, and the tremble in her voice made Sandy's stomach churn. She reached across the table and gave Dorie's hand a squeeze. Beneath the battleaxe exterior, she was a woman scared of losing her son.

"You're plenty of good, don't you dare think otherwise." Sandy said as she pushed her chair back and left Dorie to her thoughts. Running a cafe was like being a therapist. She had watched most of the villagers cry into their coffees at one point or another. It was a huge privilege really, to provide such a safe space for so many people.

Sandy's thoughts were interrupted by a scream from outside. She turned around but couldn't see what the noise was until she noticed movement across the village square.

"Oh no." Sandy said as she saw Gus Sanders land a punch on a small, unkempt man. She opened the cafe door and sprinted across the village square as quickly as she could, which wasn't very. "Gus! Gus, stop!"

The scruffy man was lying on the floor, a dirty backpack next to him. As Sandy got closer she saw that the backpack was unzipped, revealing a bright yellow tin of spray paint.

"He's had it coming! Caught him red-handed, the little sod! Standing here in broad daylight painting more rubbish on my shop!"

Sandy crouched down closer to the man, who appeared to be about her age but had a full beard that added at least 20 years on to his age. "Is that true?"

"What's it to you?" The man asked with a groan. His face was a mish-mash of bruises, not all of them fresh enough to have been caused by Gus.

"Have some respect." A voice called from behind, and

Sandy turned to see Derrick sprinting towards them. "That's no way to talk to a lady."

"Blooming Deves, hey. You one of them, now?" The man asked.

"You two know each other?" Gus asked, his face still beet red with anger and physical exertion.

"We're both staying at the Manor." Derrick explained, then looked at Sandy with concern. "Are you ok?"

"I'm fine." Sandy said.

"You're mad." Derrick said. "You don't see a fight and run over to it. You could have got hurt."

"The lad's right, Sandy, go back to your cafe and leave this to me." Gus said.

"I'm staying right here to make sure nobody else gets hurt." Sandy insisted. She didn't quite trust what Gus might do unsupervised. "We should call the police."

"The police won't do anything, I'll sort this myself." Gus said, bending down and pulling the man up by his thin t-shirt.

"Gus! Leave him!" Sandy cried, as Gus reared his arm back to prepare a punch.

"Stop it, mate." Derrick said and squeezed between the two men. Gus released the graffiti menace, who toppled back to the floor with a bang and let out a cry.

"Me back! Argh!" He moaned as he twisted into a fetal position on the floor.

"Is he ok?" Sandy asked, pulling her mobile phone out of her pocket.

"Who cares? He's no good to anyone. Squatting up there, causing trouble down here. They're no good. I'll kill them!" Gus shouted, then turned to the man on the floor and leaned over until their faces were close together. "Do you hear me? I'll kill you all!"

Gus grabbed the man's bag and stomped back into the butcher's with it.

Sandy looked at Derrick, who was standing over the man on the floor.

"He's gone." Derrick said to the man in a more stern, harsh voice than Sandy had heard him use before. "Give over with this now, get up."

"He's really hurt me, man." The man groaned.

"So he should. Get up - you're a disgrace." Derrick said, looking down at the man with disgust.

"Derrick, maybe we should call an ambulance?" Sandy asked. As a small business owner, she understood Gus' anger towards the man who had been waging a graffiti vendetta against his shop, but she couldn't leave an injured person on the floor.

"He's fine, Sandy. Let's go." Derrick said. It was the first time he'd used her name, and as he did so, he looped his arm around her shoulders and lead her away from the man on the ground.

"Gus won't really kill anyone, you know." Sandy said.

Derrick shrugged. "We'll see. He looked angry and someone has already killed one of us."

Sandy swallowed as a cold chill took over her body. "You say one of us, but I thought you were going home now you've got a job?"

"I will do." Derrick said. "I want to go back when I can give something, I can't be taking any more."

"Do you mean money?" Sandy asked, surprised at her own ignorance. "You should have said. Everyone gets paid monthly but I can give you some earlier, even pay you weekly if that would help?"

Derrick grinned. "You've already done enough for me,

lady. I don't want you to go to any trouble. I can handle a few more nights there."

"I bet your mum's excited to be getting you back home?" Sandy asked.

"I haven't seen her since I left." Derrick admitted. "I couldn't bring myself to visit. Visiting's alright but then you've gotta leave again. Easier to just pretend."

"Well, you'll be home soon." Sandy said, giving Derrick's arm a squeeze. She couldn't imagine experiencing such things at his age and choosing to sacrifice himself so his younger siblings had more. "I'll nip to the bank at lunch and sort your wages."

Derrick grinned and planted a kiss on her forehead, just as they reached the cafe.

To Sandy's surprise, Tom Nelson was standing outside. "What happened? I heard a racket but Bernice said you'd got it handled."

Sandy laughed. "Remind me to thank Bernice!"

"Sure you're ok?" Tom asked, his eyes narrowing with concern.

Sandy felt her cheeks burn. "I'm fine, but Gus has caught the graffiti artist."

"Ouch." Tom said, smiling to reveal a perfect dimple in his cheek. "I can guess who came off worse."

"He's going to kill all the squatters." Derrick said, raising his eyebrows in exclamation. "I'm late for work, see you in there Sandy."

He walked into the cafe and left Sandy standing with Tom, who was gazing at her as he had on quiz night.

"Well, I should, I should get back too." Sandy stuttered, pointing behind her to the cafe door, where she knew Coral and probably half of the customers would be watching her and gossiping.

"Did he really say he'd kill them?" Tom asked.

Sandy nodded. "I'll kill you all. They were his exact words."

"Geeze." Tom said, shaking his head. "We should tell Poppy."

Sandy felt her heart race at there being a 'we' that comprised her and Tom Nelson. "Yes, we definitely should."

"Shall we see her together? I could nip out this evening. You might already have plans?"

"No, no. I could do that." Sandy said. "You don't think he might mean it, do you, Tom?"

Tom gazed across the square at the butcher's and Sandy followed his gaze. The pavement was empty now, the graffiti menace must have recovered enough to hobble away. As they watched, Gus appeared at the shop door in his blue and white striped apron and stared across to his right, towards Waterfell Manor.

"I don't know." Tom said. "I really don't know."

9

*T*om Nelson insisted on picking Sandy up from home.

She spent 30 minutes lounging in a scaldingly hot bath reading her latest mystery novel, and that left her with not enough time to get ready.

She dried herself quickly and gave her hair a quick straighten, then considered her reflection in the mirror. She was clueless about makeup really and wished she'd asked Cass to come over and do it for her.

But, it wasn't a date, and Tom Nelson had seen her often enough to notice if she appeared looking like a drag queen. She didn't want to appear too keen.

They were just acquaintances who were both concerned about a friend. The evening was an act of civic duty really, not romance.

With that thought in mind, she applied some blusher to her cheeks and a coat of mascara to her eyelashes, then pouted her lips and applied a baby pink lipgloss.

"That'll do." She said to her reflection. With that, she sat and waited in her cosy living room, sneaking in another few pages of her book.

She was impressed when a knock at her front door came at exactly 7pm, and tried to ignore the flutter in her chest.

"Nice place!" Tom said by way of a greeting, as Sandy opened the door. He was dressed as he always was, in a checked shirt and faded jeans. He looked incredibly handsome.

"Oh, thanks. Do you want to come in?" Sandy asked, hoping her question appeared as the polite offer it was and not as a flirtatious remark. "While I grab my coat?"

"Sure." Tom said, smiling at her. He followed her into the living room and, to her surprise, went straight to the fire-place and examined the photographs on the mantelpiece.

"Make yourself at home." Sandy said. "Do you want a drink?"

"Well, what are we doing?" Tom asked, turning to face her. "Are we going to see Poppy? We could have a drink after?"

"Good plan." Sandy said, annoyed with herself for being so jittery. Her mum had always taught her that expressing an emotion removed its power, so she tested it out. "I'm really nervous, sorry."

"Hey, don't be." He said, moving closer to her. "I can do the talking if you want? It'll be okay. Poppy needs to know."

Sandy nodded. "You're right. Let's do it."

The two left the house and Tom drove them across the village, past the police station, to the terraced home where Gus and Poppy Sanders lived. Tom parked up on the pavement outside the house, which was in darkness.

"Looks like they're out?" Sandy said.

"Gus will be." Tom said, climbing out of the car door. "Come on."

Sandy followed Tom up the small path to the front door, where he knocked three times. The door opened, and Poppy appeared in a chunky cardigan and leggings. She grinned at Tom and wrapped her arms around him, and Sandy felt her stomach churn with jealousy.

"Oh!" Poppy exclaimed, noticing Sandy standing behind Tom. "You're together? Come in."

Sandy noticed how her presence made Poppy appear less relaxed, but she followed Poppy into the house. Poppy lead them into the front living room, which was more old-fashioned than Sandy had imagined. Above the fireplace was a cabinet filled with guns.

"Wow, are those real?" Sandy asked, standing and looking at them. She had never seen a real gun before, and even being in a room with them made her feel nervous.

Poppy laughed. "They are. Gus likes to think he's a hunter-gatherer or something. It's locked, don't worry. So, this is a surprise, what can I do for you both?"

"It's about Gus." Tom began. Sandy noted how at home he seemed as he sprawled across one of the floral-patterned settees. She took a seat in a single armchair and left the talking to Tom.

"What's he done now?" Poppy asked, sitting in the other single chair without offering them drinks.

"More fighting." Tom said. "And this time he's threatened to kill someone... well, several people."

"And you saw this, did you?" Poppy asked, looking right at Sandy.

"I did." Sandy said. "Hasn't he told you about it?"

"He won't have been home yet." Tom said. The intimacy between him and Poppy made Sandy uncomfortable. "Am I right?"

Poppy sighed. "He won't be long. Tom, you've got to stop this, he's my husband."

"And you deserve better." Tom said.

Sandy stood up. "I'm going to leave you two to it, I don't think I need to be here."

"Oh, don't go, Sandy." Poppy said. "My brother is a little over protective of me, that's all."

"Your brother?" Sandy asked.

"Poppy's my little sister, didn't you know that?" Tom asked.

"No... no, I didn't." Sandy said, laughing at her own foolishness. The revelation highlighted how little she knew Tom Nelson and how silly she had been to imagine the evening as being any more than a way of him finding an unbiased person to share his opinion of Gus Sanders. "Poppy, Gus caught someone graffitiing today. There was a scuffle, and Gus threatened to kill all of the squatters."

Poppy's face blanched. "He really said that?"

Sandy nodded.

Poppy sighed. "I can't believe he'd be so stupid when there's just been a murder."

"You've got your job to think about." Tom urged. "The school won't want a teacher's husband going around the village threatening to kill people."

"It's just words, Tom, you know what he's like when he gets angry. And the graffiti has nearly ruined his business! He would never hurt anyone."

"Poppy, are you listening? Sandy had to split up a fight he was having. He has hurt someone! And only stopped because a woman interrupted him."

"I'll deal with it." Poppy said. She stood up. "I need to be on my own for a bit. I appreciate you coming and telling me, but I need to be alone."

Sandy and Tom stood up and saw themselves out of the house. They stood together at the side of Tom's car.

"You really didn't know she was my sister?" Tom asked after a few moments.

Sandy laughed. "I don't think I know much at all about you, really."

"Well, we can't have that." Tom said, flashing her his winning smile - and dimple. "How about that drink?"

"Sure." Sandy said, not wanting to risk the gossip mill by going to The Tweed. "I've got a bottle of wine at mine, fancy it?"

"Sounds good." Tom said. "Let's have a drive first, though, is that OK?"

"Yeah, sure." Sandy said. They climbed into the car and Tom drove out of the village and into the Peak District. The scenery was beautiful, and Sandy sat back and looked out of the window.

"I love driving around." Tom said after a few minutes of happy silence. "Just heading off with nowhere to go, see where I end up."

"What do you do, when you're not running The Tweed?" Sandy asked. "I never see you in the cafe."

"Sorry about that." Tom said. "I have to be careful with what I eat. All I have to do is look through your window and I put weight on."

Sandy laughed. "I know what you mean. It can be dangerous for the waistline, running a cake shop."

"I keep meaning to come in now there's more books." Tom admitted. "I love books. Just need to see if I can race by the cake counter unhurt."

Sandy laughed again. "Good luck with that. What books do you like?"

"Never met one I don't like. I read the classics, I even like some poetry believe it or not."

"Really?" Sandy asked in surprise.

"I know! I mean, I don't read as much as I used to. I sleep in late, my sleep pattern's pretty messed up. That's what running a pub will do for you."

"I'm the opposite. Up early."

"Yeah, you've got to have all the food ready before you open, that must be a killer."

"Not really, I like being the first one up. The village is so quiet and peaceful."

"I bet I'm only in bed an hour before you wake up." Tom said as they drove to an elevated point overlooking a beautiful valley. Tom parked the car and looked at Sandy. "Ever been here before?"

Sandy looked out into the darkness and squinted. "I don't think so?"

"It's Black Rock. The views here in the day are amazing. We must come some time." Tom said.

"I'd like that." Sandy admitted, feeling her cheeks flush. "Can we have a look now too?"

"Sure thing." Tom said, and they each got out of the car. Tom walked across to Sandy and took her hand in his. "Hold on, it's a sudden drop, we don't want to go too close."

"Ok." Sandy breathed, her heart racing with the feeling of her fingers being linked through Tom's.

"Hey, I never got to ask what it was like to solve a murder case." Tom said.

Sandy shook her head. "I've put all that behind me."

"Really? I thought you'd have a theory about this homeless man's hit and run."

Sandy took a deep breath. "I guess I've learned that I like a quiet life. I'm letting the police do their job."

Tom grinned. "Hopefully they don't hear about Gus."

"Do you not like him?"

"Argh... I don't dislike him. He's fine. My sister can't see any bad in him and that drives me mad because he finishes work and goes straight to the pub every night, leaving her sitting in darkness at home. But that doesn't make him a murderer."

"Hmm." Sandy murmured.

"I'd probably be just as angry as he is, to be honest if someone did that outside my pub."

"Me too." Sandy blurted. "Outside my cafe, I mean."

Tom laughed. "Let's get back for that wine, it's too cold up here."

They got back in the car and sank into a comfortable silence, each one lost in their thoughts. Sandy flexed her fingers, noticing how her hand felt strange and empty without Tom holding it. She shook her head; he had been keeping her safe from the drop, that's all.

After a few short minutes of driving through peaceful country roads and winding lanes, the familiar sign greeted them announcing that they were entering Waterfell Tweed.

Please drive safely through our village! The sign requested.

"That's a bit ironic now, isn't it?" Tom said, also noticing the sign.

"Yeah, it is." Sandy said.

"What's going on up there?" Tom asked as they reached the village square. A dark shape was stood in the middle of the road, facing them. The person had their arms outstretched upwards, and appeared to be screaming for help that was not coming. A dark shape lay in the road in front of the person.

"Isn't that..." Sandy began, thinking she recognised the silent screamer.

Tom stopped the car and unbuckled his seat belt. "Have you got a phone? We might need to call for help."

They both jumped out of his car and walked towards the scene.

"Hello?" Sandy called.

"Help?" A familiar voice called. "There's been another murder! Help!"

10

"*We* can only tell next of kin." Jim Slaughter explained from behind the custody desk of the police station. "I'm sorry Sandy, it's resources, cost-cutting, you know."

"I understand." Sandy said. If the police wouldn't share the news, she would have to. She had given her statement to the police and expected Tom to be waiting for her in the station after having given his, but he was gone. Sandy tried not to be disappointed.

She said goodbye to Jim and trudged out of the station, feeling silly with her rosy cheeks and made-up eyes. Then, she avoided the High Street, which was still cordoned off in places, and continued instead down Water Lane, past the hair salon and the bakers and the Chinese takeaway on the corner, past the vet's and the row of terraced houses until she reached the house she wanted.

She gazed at it, taking a deep breath, then opened the wooden gate and walked up the short path before rapping at the door. The house was in darkness, it was almost midnight, and there was no noise for a few moments, then

Sandy heard the stomping of feet racing down the stairs. A bleary-eyed Cass opened the door, a fluffy dressing gown wrapped around her.

"What's wrong?" She asked, holding the door open. "Do you know what time it is?"

"I need to talk to Olivia." Sandy said.

"Now?" Cass asked.

"Yeah... It can't wait. I don't want her to hear it from anyone else." Sandy said, fighting back her own tears.

"Oh my God, what is it?" Cass asked, collapsing onto the second step of the stairs.

A noise from the top of the stairs made them both look up. Standing at the top of the staircase, dressed in an oversized tee shirt, stood Olivia.

"Olivia... come down." Sandy asked, noticing that her own teeth were chattering.

"What's wrong, Auntie Sandy?" Olivia asked, walking down the stairs as asked.

"Let's go in the living room." Sandy said, knowing the house like the back of her hand. She lead the three of them into the living room, where she sat on the floor and crossed her legs. Olivia looked at Cass and frowned, then copied. Cass stifled a yawn and joined the two of them on the floor.

"I've got some bad news." Sandy began. "There's been another accident, another hit and run, tonight."

"That's awful." Olivia said, her age protecting her from any sense that the news may affect her.

"Who was hit?" Cass asked.

"It was Derrick." Sandy said, and a shiver ran up her body as she thought back to recognising the figure on the ground as being her newest employee.

"No!" Olivia wailed, jumping up from the floor and pacing the room. "You're lying!"

"I'm not lying, Olivia. I wanted to tell you myself... I know you're close to him."

"Is he dead?" Olivia asked.

Sandy took a breath. "No. He's in hospital, but he was very badly hurt, Olivia. He might not pull through."

"He has to." Olivia said, then turned her gaze to Cass. "We need to see him."

Cass nodded. "I'll get dressed."

Olivia pounded up the stairs, Cass following behind in a daze. Sandy followed her up the stairs and sat on her unmade bed as she pulled on some leggings and a dark jumper.

"Who did this?" Cass asked, her voice thick with emotion. "Who could mow down an innocent teenager?"

Sandy thought back to Gus' threat earlier in the day. "I don't know."

"Don't you want to find out?" Cass asked. "You're good at this, Sandy, you could help the police. Someone has to stop this happening."

Sandy watched her friend but said nothing. She had given the police days to make progress on the case and couldn't bear the thought that her actions - or lack of - had put Derrick in grave danger.

"Come on, let's go." Olivia said, appearing in the doorway in an outfit almost identical to the one Cass was wearing.

"I'll come with you." Sandy said.

The journey across town was in silence. If Olivia had questions, she chose not to ask them, and Sandy had no energy to make polite small talk. Her body was bone tired, her mind racing with adrenaline. She felt as if she was experiencing some kind of bizarre jetlag.

The hospital was a buzz of activity, with doctors and

nurses milling around, patients being woken to have their vitals checked yet again, and the few visitors who hadn't gone home pacing the corridors. Olivia and Cass were shown into Derrick's room, where his body was hooked up to wires and machines, and Sandy took a seat outside.

With nothing but time, she pulled out her small notebook from her handbag and wrote ANTON and DERRICK in large letters, then drew a line connecting them. The connection seemed obvious; they were both squatters.

The word made her wince. If only she had thought things through more, she would have realised that Derrick would return home as soon as he had some wages to take. She could have paid him daily and then he would have left the village after work each night - she might have even driven him. He wouldn't have been hanging around the village square to be run over, and he wouldn't have been a squatter anymore to be at risk.

The prime suspect was Ignatius Potter, so Sandy wrote his name on her sheet with a question mark. DC Sullivan had taken no one else in for questioning since he returned to the village.

And yet, he had an alibi. Dorie Slaughter had been with him until moments before he discovered Anton's body.

Sandy rubbed her temples and scribbled on the page, IS DORIE'S ALIBI RELIABLE?

Writing the words made her feel guilty, but Dorie was getting older. Could she have muddled the days or times in her mind? Had the police taken her statement and decided it was unreliable?

Whoever was targeting the squatters must have a reason - a motive. Sandy scrawled the word MOTIVE on the piece of paper.

Seeing her thoughts spread out helped her mind whir with ideas.

Why would someone want to kill squatters?

She remembered Gus Sanders' threat. His promise to kill all of the squatters. She wrote his name on the paper.

Seeing the names of two people she knew, even if not well, on her pad as suspects, made her shiver, and she put the book back in her handbag.

Clearly, she would have to investigate further.

**

After sitting by Derrick's hospital bed for hours, Cass convinced Olivia that they needed to return home for some sleep. The doctors gave little information, appearing at regular intervals to make checks and speak in vague terms.

He's sustained very serious injuries. He's stable. The next few hours are crucial.

Sandy sat in the back seat of Cass' car as they drove back in an exhausted silence. The sun was rising.

"Are you coming in?" Cass asked as they all climbed out of the car outside her little house. "I don't think I'll sleep."

"Yeah, sure." Sandy said, following her friend up the garden path.

The house was cold and all three of them pulled their clothes around them tighter as they walked in.

"Go on up to bed." Cass instructed Olivia as she turned the thermostat up. The radiators groaned and hissed as they woke up. "Have as long as you need, I won't wake you."

Olivia walked upstairs without responding or saying goodnight. She seemed in a daze.

"How is she?" Sandy asked. She had walked straight

through to the kitchen and filled the kettle with water to make strong coffees for them both.

Cass shrugged and cried. "He looks so fragile. It's awful seeing someone so young and healthy lying there like that."

Sandy nodded as she carried two steaming cups of coffee into the living room, where Cass was sitting on the settee under a blanket. Sandy sat next to her, close enough that their legs touched, and pulled some of the blanket over herself. "I can't believe this has happened."

"What are the police even doing? Do they have any suspects?" Cass asked, drinking her coffee without even seeming to notice it was scalding hot.

"They're focused on Ignatius Potter."

"So it was him?" Cass asked.

"No." Sandy said, the thought only just hitting her. "He couldn't have hurt Derrick. His car was seized after Anton's death."

"Great." Cass said. "So there's a killer on the loose and the police have no idea who it is."

"I'm sure they're working on it." Sandy said. "I haven't heard much about the investigation this time."

Their conversation was interrupted by a soft sobbing coming from upstairs. Sandy and Cass looked at each other.

"Shall we go up?" Sandy asked.

"No." Cass said. "She doesn't like people seeing her upset. She'll come down if she wants to."

"As if she hasn't been through enough already." Sandy muttered.

Cass let out a huge yawn.

"Come on, why don't we get some sleep." Sandy said, leaning her body to the left and pulling Cass across with her so they were curled into each other across the settee. They'd slept the same way many times over the years, to comfort each other about relationships ending and bad days at work. They'd spent weeks sleeping the same way when Sandy's mother had died, with Coral piled into the jumble of bodies with them.

Within seconds, Cass' breath slowed and she fell into a deep sleep. Cass' sleep was always deep. Sandy closed her eyes but sleep evaded her. Instead, she pictured Derrick, running to her aid as she tried to calm Gus Sanders down.

Was it Derrick's involvement that day that made Gus target him?

And why had Ignatius Potter discovered both bodies? Could a man really be so unlucky?

11

*I*t was a strange day in the cafe without Derrick helping.

Even though he had only been working for Sandy for a few days, he was so grateful for the opportunity and eager to prove himself that he did much more work than anyone expected him to - and with a bigger smile than anyone washing dishes might have been expected to have.

"Oh, love." Bernice said as Sandy walked into the cafe soon after opening time. Bernice scooped her into a hug.

"It's so awful."Sandy nodded. "I was there overnight."

"Have you slept at all? You look exhausted." Bernice asked, pulling back from the hug and holding Sandy by her elbows as she looked deep into her eyes.

"I've had a couple of hours. I might not be much use today." She admitted.

"That's fine. I couldn't sleep so I came in extra early. The baking's all done. You take it easy." Bernice said.

"Thank you so much." Sandy said, feeling tearful. She didn't know what she had done to deserve such loyal employees, and friends.

The cafe was already full and bustling with the sharing of gossip from table to table.

"My Jim will solve the case." Dorie Slaughter said, taking centre court from a table right in the middle of the cafe. "He interviewed the prime suspect."

"I thought you gave that prime suspect an alibi?" Sandy asked.

"Well, yes, but he was the prime suspect from the information my Jim had." Dorie said. Sandy rolled her eyes. She worried that Dorie's adoration for her son clouded most other things, including catching the real killer if it meant suggesting that her son had been wrong.

"You went and made a statement, didn't you Dorie?" Sandy pressed as she pulled her apron on. She would remain downstairs for the day, where she could listen to what people were saying and begin her own investigations.

Dorie gave a loud sigh. "I'm not incapable, you know. You young folk always assume nobody else knows like you do."

Sandy felt her cheeks flush and was about to apologise when Dorie stood up and pulled her coat and Russian hat on.

"Best be off!" Dorie called.

"You didn't give the statement, did you?"

"Well... I was going to, but I got distracted."

Sandy tutted. "Well don't get distracted again Dorie, go on. Come back after and I'll make you a fresh tea."

Dorie gave a thumbs up in agreement and raced off out of the cafe.

"She's mad." Coral said, emerging at the back of the cafe from the staircase with a plate and cup in her hands. "Did you know people are taking drinks up there? And food!"

"No..." Sandy said. "I didn't know."

"We'll put a sign up." Bernice said, always quick to find a solution to a problem.

"Thanks, Bernice." Sandy said.

"How's Derrick?" Coral asked, on her way to drop the dirty dishes into the overflowing sink. "You can tell he's not here."

"They say he's stable." Sandy said, speaking so that the customers would hear. She studied each person, in turn, to see if anyone looked disappointed with that news, but most were too busy sharing their own theories to react to her words at all.

"That's good."

"Hopefully. He's a young fit lad, maybe he can pull through."

The doorbell rang and Tom Nelson appeared, his face harried with concern. Sandy still hadn't heard from him since the night before and was disappointed that he hadn't texted to check she was ok.

"Sandy! Thank goodness!" He exclaimed, and she noticed that he was still in the same clothes from the night before. She had at least had a shower and borrowed some clothes at Cass' house. "I've been worried sick."

"Worried?" She asked as she noticed the customers watching the interaction. "Come through here."

Sandy led Tom through the cafe tables and up the staircase to the first floor, where a few people were too busy with their noses in books to pay any attention to her.

"What happened to you? I waited in the station after giving my statement but you must have already gone. You didn't even text me." Sandy said, trying her best not to sound like a possessive girlfriend to a man she wasn't even dating.

"Sandy..." He began. "I don't even have your number."

The ridiculousness of her upset caused her to let out a high-pitched laugh. A stranger who was browsing the theology section turned and scowled at her.

"Of course you don't. I'm sorry, I just thought you'd wait for me."

"I did wait for you, Sandy. I was there half the night wondering what on earth they were doing to you. Then DC Sullivan popped his head out and asked what I was loitering around for! Said you'd gone hours earlier. So I went to your house to see if you were ok, and there was no answer."

"Oh!" Sandy said, realising what a mix up it had been. "I went to see Cass. I told Olivia what had happened."

"Who's Olivia?" "Her sister. She's Derrick's girlfriend."

"Oh wow. How did that go?"

"Rough... as you'd imagine. We went to the hospital and stayed there most of the night, then I stayed there until I came into work." Sandy said. "You haven't been looking for me all night, have you?"

"No." Tom said in a whisper, then leaned towards her. "I went to check on Poppy and, guess what, Gus didn't make it home last night."

"You're kidding?"

"No. I stayed up with Poppy all night, trying to get to the bottom of things. We must have rung his phone a hundred times, no answer."

A chill ran down Sandy's back. She turned and looked out of the window across the village square, towards the butcher's, and couldn't believe her eyes.

"Oh, my." She exclaimed, covering her hand with her mouth. A group of at least 50 people, all in various states of disarray, many carrying sleeping bags on their backs and carrier bags in their hands, were trudging across the square.

"They're on the move." Tom said, standing so close

behind Sandy she could feel his presence. "Can't say I blame them."

"I need to do something." Sandy said, pushing past Tom and racing downstairs. "Bernice! Box up as much hot food as we've got ready!"

All of the cafe customers were gawping out of the windows at the sight of 50 homeless men, women and children crossing the village square.

"Wait!" Sandy called to them, opening the cafe door. The man who was leading the group turned and looked at her in disgust.

"Wait why?"

"I want to help you. Please just wait a few minutes, I can make hot bacon sandwiches for you all."

"We don't want your help." A younger man sneered, and Sandy recognised him as being the graffiti artist who Gus had attacked.

"But where are you going?"

"Somewhere safe." A woman called, falling out of line to address Sandy. A young boy clung to her legs.

"Please let me help." Sandy said. "Your son, let me give him some food."

The boy was practically climbing up the woman's body. His body was painfully thin.

"Get me to cross over so you can run me over, is that it?" The woman asked although she was moving closer as the rest of the group continued to walk on.

"I only want to help. I promise." Sandy said.

"Come on, here's a bacon sandwich for you each." Tom said, appearing behind her. He had a brown bag in each hand and strode out across the street towards the woman and her child. "Spread the word, we've got plenty more."

The boy snatched a brown bag from Tom and then

returned to hiding as close as he could to his mother, who held out her own hand more warily.

"Do you have somewhere to go?" Sandy asked.

The woman shrugged and followed the rest of the group. "We'll find somewhere."

**

"Wow." Sandy said as she stood on the doorstep with Tom a few moments later. "I never imagined there would be children up there. I know that sounds silly... if a man and woman become homeless there's every chance they'll have a child."

"You're a good person, Sandy." Tom said. "Everyone else has watched those people go by and let them."

"I gave out two bacon sandwiches." Sandy said. "I've hardly saved the world."

"But you've tried, at least." Tom said with a smile. "In fact, you've inspired me. I'm going to go up to the Manor, see if anyone's still there. Take a few sandwiches, that kind of thing."

"I'll come with you." Sandy said, then regretted her forwardness. "If that's OK, I mean."

"Of course." Tom said with a grin.

They each spent ten minutes gathering food and met outside The Tweed, where they loaded Tom's boot and drove across the square towards the Manor. As they pulled onto the gravel in front of the building, Sandy noticed movement from the side of the building. "There's someone over there!"

"Hello!" Tom called, as he climbed out of the car. Sandy

copied and ran around to his side, standing close to him. "Hello?"

A small shape appeared, their feet crunching through the gravel as they walked. "Is that -" Sandy began.

"Sandy? Tom Nelson?" The woman asked, moving closer to them.

"Pritti?" Sandy asked. "What are you doing here?"

"I'm doing my job now those people have gone!" Pritti said, then turned on her heels and returned down the side of the building. Sandy and Tom looked at each other and shrugged, then followed Pritti.

The Manor was incredible from afar, sitting on an elevated bluff over the village, but it was only up close that it was possible to realise just how large it was. Standing so close to its walls made Sandy feel tiny. Pritti was working up ahead, a bin liner in one hand and a grabbing claw in the other. The gravel and grass were littered with beer cans and food packaging. Sandy watched as Pritti attempted to grab a used nappy with the claw.

"Did the squatters make this mess?" Sandy asked.

Pritti turned to look at her as she got the nappy in the bin liner. "Of course they did. They have no respect. That's why they had to go."

"How did you get them to leave?" Tom asked, looking at the woman's tiny frame.

"I didn't, they decided it was time to move on."

"Someone's killing them one by one, that's why they're moving on." Tom said, but Pritti had returned to her litter picking. Sandy glanced at Tom.

"We should go."

Tom shrugged. "If we loop through the village we might find the squatters. Maybe we could still hand out the food."

"Is the Manor empty now?" Sandy called. "Have they all gone?"

"Every last one." Pritti said as she picked up an empty carrier bag."Okay... well, we'll leave you to it." Sandy said. Pritti didn't appear to hear. "Bye!"

"Bye, Mrs. Sharma." Tom said. Pritti held up a hand half-heartedly in farewell, as she surveyed the work left to be done.

"Can you imagine being that committed to your work?" Tom asked as they got back in the car. "Her bosses aren't even in the country and she's out in the cold picking up dirty nappies."

"I guess nobody else will do it." Sandy said. "Anyway, tell me more about Gus. Where do you think he was?"

Tom sighed. "He stays out late, Sandy. A lot. But he always comes home at some point. Poppy was beside herself."

"I bet she was." Sandy said. Poppy was such a kind, gentle soul. She didn't deserve to be put through worry like that.

The car reached the end of the Manor's driveway, and Tom turned left past the church. Sandy kept her gaze focused on her side of the road and tried to look into the butchers. It was in darkness.

"I went there before I came to your cafe." Tom explained. "He should be open today but it's all in darkness. I thought I'll give him until 9am, then 10am, then lunch... he is my brother in law, after all. But I need to go to the police at some point."

"And tell them about the argument?"

"The fight. Yes." Tom corrected.

"Does Poppy know you're going to do that?"

"She will do. I didn't tell her, but she's a bright girl, and she knows what the right thing to do is. He threatened to kill squatters and then a squatter was run over and he's done a runner. It seems straightforward."

"Hmm." Sandy murmured.

"What?"

"I always think things that seem that straightforward probably aren't, but maybe I'm being naive. I mean, the police arrested Ignatius Potter and said it seemed like an open and shut case."

"And then he discovered the second body. Poor guy." Tom said.

"I keep thinking, I wonder if there's a reason that he has discovered both bodies?"

"Well, it's because he's guilty or he's really unlucky."

"Or he could be being framed." Sandy said, thinking back to her own experience of Reginald Halfman being murdered.

"If he's being framed, he has to have a motive to make it realistic it could be him."

"The motive's easy on this." Sandy said with some confidence. "Someone wants to get rid of the squatters.. and, it's mission accomplished."

"I don't think that's the motive." Tom said. They were driving through country lanes, looking out for a crowd of homeless people, but the streets were deserted. "And I don't think we're going to find anyone now."

"Yeah, I think you're right." Sandy agreed. "But how can you think that isn't the motive?"

"Well, it is part of the motive, but it's not all of it. Yes, someone wants to get rid of the squatters - but why?"

"Well..." Sandy said but stopped herself.

"Go on, you can say it."

"Well, if it is Gus, it's revenge."

12

"*A*h! Here she is!" Sandy exclaimed as Dorie Slaughter barged back into the cafe. It was several hours after she had left in a hurry to attend the police station, and in that time the wind had begun to howl and the sky had darkened. There was a storm on the way.

"I'll take that tea you promised," Dorie said, taking a seat at the table closest to the counter. The cafe had grown quiet in the last half an hour. Parents had looked at their watches and left to do the school run.

"Coming right up," Sandy said, turning her back on Dorie to make the drink.

"Shall I package you a slice to take home?" Coral asked as she rang in Elaine Peters' order in the till. "You enjoyed it last time, didn't you?"

"Go on then, Coral," Elaine said with a smile. "I'm not sure how good for my waistline it is coming in here."

"You need to be careful too," Dorie called. "My Jim likes a slim woman."

Elaine's cheeks flushed.

"Dorie! I'm sure Jim likes Elaine exactly as she is."

Sandy said, realising after she'd finished that it was perhaps a back-handed compliment.

"He's got a few pounds to lose himself, anyway. That police uniform's getting tight on him." Coral said, with a wink.

"He's a perfect specimen." Dorie cried. "And anyway, it's a woman's job to feed her man. He should be putting weight on if Elaine is doing things right."

"I'll be going now," Elaine said, without waiting for an extra slice of cake to be cut. "Nice to see you all."

Sandy watched her leave, the wind blowing her hair in all directions as she raced across the High Street. "You should be nice to her, Dorie, she's a lovely match for your Jim."

"Hmm," Dorie grumbled. "Do you know she buys grated cheese?"

"What's that got to do with anything?" Coral asked.

"Grated cheese!" Dorie repeated as if that would make things clear.

"We buy grated cheese here," Sandy said.

"Why am I not surprised," Dorie said, with a roll of her eyes.

"You know, Dorie, Mr. Potter told me you'd been looking at moving," Sandy said, taking the strong-smelling tea across to Dorie's table and sitting down next to her. "You know we'd all miss you if you left, don't you?"

"Of course I do!" Dorie exclaimed. "But I can't spend my whole life pleasing everyone else."

"No, no, of course not. What does Jim think of the idea?"

"How would I know? I never see him anymore."

"I bet he's busy with the murder case," Sandy said, deciding to flatter the woman's ego to get her on side.

"You've done such a good job raising our best police officer, it's not surprising he's in demand."

"Well, maybe it's time he flew the nest," Dorie said, as she lifted the mug to take a sip of tea. Sandy had been serving her so long, she knew exactly how strong to make the drink for her. Dorie Slaughter was a Waterfell Tweed institution, and with Benedict and Penelope Harlow away, Sandy realised that the thought of losing Dorie as well made her sad.

"Don't make any rash decisions, hey. You're my best customer, remember." Sandy said, giving the woman's hand a squeeze as she stood up and returned to the counter.

The noise of the wind could be heard even in the cafe, and Sandy's thoughts turned to the group of people who would be searching for safe cover for the night. She wished she had been able to give more of them a hot meal earlier.

The doorbell rang and Jim Slaughter didn't so much walk in as get thrown in by the gale.

"Hello, Jim," Sandy said to him quietly. "We've just been talking about you. I think your mum's missing you a bit."

Jim glanced across in his mother's direction, smoothing his tie down over his protruding stomach. "Ah, thanks. I guess I have been neglecting her a bit."

"Jim!" Dorie called, spotting him. "Come and sit down, Sandy can get you a drink. Sandy, bring a hot chocolate for my son."

Sandy smiled at Jim. "Hot chocolate?"

"Sounds good." Jim said, grinning. He smelt sweaty, and Sandy wondered how he had managed to sweat on such a cold day. "It's been a mad day."

"At least you managed to take your mum's statement." Sandy said. "She meant to give it days ago."

"Well, that was a waste of time," Jim said. "Decision's been made just now on it."

"What decision?"

Jim looked behind him to the door. "I shouldn't say but you'll hear all about it later. Ignatius Potter has been charged with the murder of Anton Carmichael and the attempted murder of Derrick Deves."

Sandy dropped the cup she was about to fill with hot chocolate, and the white ceramic smashed into small slices across the floor. The noise brought Coral from the kitchen, where she and Bernice were trying to keep up with the dish-washing in Derrick's absence.

"That's impossible." Sandy said.

"DC Sullivan made the call." Jim said with a shrug. It was clear he was being shut out of yet another Waterfell Tweed case by the city police.

"But Mr. Potter didn't even have a car when Derrick was run over. He couldn't have done it."

Jim shrugged once more.

"This is ridiculous," Sandy said, opening the counter hatch and grabbing her coat from the stand.

"Where are you going?" Bernice called.

"I'm going to sort out this mess."

**

In just the few moments it took Sandy to walk from her cafe to the police station, she was frozen to the core. The wind was bitter, hitting her bare face and feeling like punches to her skin.

She stomped into the police station, which was empty.

"Hello!" She shouted, pacing the length of the reception

area for a good few minutes until she heard movement from behind the desk.

"Sandy Shaw, well hello." DC Sullivan said, standing with his arms crossed. "Have you brought a cake?"

"No, I have not. I need to speak to you, now." Sandy said, her firmness surprising even her. DC Sullivan raised an eyebrow and disappeared, appearing from a door in reception a few moments later.

"Does this need to be on record?" DC Sullivan asked. "Shall I set up the recorder?"

"No, I need to speak to you about Ignatius Potter."

DC Sullivan sighed and opened the door to a small, informal room. There were two settees with a coffee table in between them, and a vending machine in the corner.

"Drink?" DC Sullivan offered.

"Not from there," Sandy said, turning her nose up as DC Sullivan pressed a button on the machine and it spat out a weak coffee for him.

"We don't all have the luxury of artisan coffees." DC Sullivan said, collecting his polystyrene cup and sitting on the settee opposite her.

"What is this room?" Sandy asked.

"It's where we speak to victims. It's meant to put people at ease, feel like a living room. As much as anywhere can in a police station."

Sandy nodded. "Well, I'm not a victim. I know that you've charged Ignatius Potter..."

"How did you hear that?" DC Sullivan asked. A burst of lavender scent wooshed out of a plug-in air freshener.

"That doesn't matter," Sandy said, not wanting to get Jim Slaughter in trouble.

"I'm guessing you're not here to congratulate me on solving the case?" DC Sullivan said with a sigh. He leaned back into the settee and took a slurp of his coffee, pulling a face as he swallowed.

"You've got the wrong man."

"We'll let the Court decide that."

"No!" Sandy cried. "This is a man's life! Will you at least hear me out?"

"Go on then." DC Sullivan said, crossing his legs and revealing striped socks underneath his trousers.

"Ignatius Potter has an alibi on the night of Anton Carmichael's death. He was with Dorie Slaughter. He could not have killed Anton. And Derrick Deves was ran over. Ignatius Potter didn't even have a car when that happened. You have his car!" Sandy said, gesturing with her hands. She had to get the officer to see that she was right.

"The fact that we have a person's car doesn't mean they can't still drive." DC Sullivan said.

"But you have his car!"

DC Sullivan smiled. A condescending smile that made Sandy want to scream. "Sandy, how many cars does Ignatius Potter have?"

"What?" Sandy asked.

"I thought as much. You've come in here, taking up my time, with your theories about what has and hasn't happened. But you're not a police officer. Why don't you leave this to the professionals, hey?" DC Sullivan said as he stood up. Sandy remained on the settee, refusing to give up so easily.

"How many cars does he have?" She forced herself to ask.

"He has at least three." DC Sullivan said. "He's quite the collector. One of them, the one used to run over Anton Carmichael, was indeed seized by us. But only that one."

"But I saw him, he was standing over Derrick Deves,

there wasn't a car in sight." Julia said, hearing her voice become desperate. She had no idea that Ignatius Potter collected cars, but then why would she?

"His car was parked outside the chip shop." DC Sullivan said. "He ran over Derrick Deves and then walked back to the scene."

"But why would someone do that? Surely he'd get out of there as quick as he could?"

DC Sullivan shrugged. "My job isn't to understand a crime, Sandy. It's just to find the person who did it. And trust me, I have found the right man."

"I just can't..." Sandy began.

"Unless!" DC Sullivan exclaimed, pacing the length of the room. "Unless you know that it was someone else, of course."

Sandy stared at the table in front of her, thinking of Gus Sanders. Thinking of his threat and his mysterious disappearance.

"I thought not." DC Sullivan said, and Sandy stood up and allowed herself to be lead out of the police station.

"I'm sorry to take up your time." Sandy said as she stood in the reception area again.

"It's okay." DC Sullivan said. "I actually kind of like it. In the city, nobody gets this involved with my cases. I wondered when you'd turn up. And hey, Sandy, next time you come, bring me a cup of proper coffee, yeah?"

Sandy gave a small nod, then braved the cold air.

She didn't return to the cafe, not wanting to face anyone.

She considered the small amount that she did know about Ignatius Potter. Could DC Sullivan be right?

Tom's words returned to her, his warning that she was only considering part of the motive for the attacks.

Why would Ignatius Potter want the squatters dead, she wondered, as she strolled through the village square. The Manor loomed ahead, elevated above the village. In the dark, without a single light on, it almost looked menacing.

And then, as she strolled slowly around the perimeter of the village square, it came to her.

Could Ignatius Potter, who owned a large proportion of the Waterfell Tweed buildings, have seen the departure of the Harlows as his chance to add the Manor to his portfolio? What a great addition to any collector's collection.

Until the squatters had arrived.

13

*A*s Sandy passed the library (closed as usual), an uneasy feeling settled in her stomach.

Ignatius Potter had acted innocent.

He'd discovered Anton's body and called for help. He's remained in the village while under suspicion. And even being the prime suspect hadn't been enough to stop him calling for help for Derrick, something that Sandy hoped might save his life.

Surely a guilty person would run?

Like Gus Sanders, Sandy thought, and a chill ran down her spine.

She turned on her heels and crossed the road again, barging her way into The Tweed. Tom Nelson was clearing glasses from an empty booth table and smiled when he saw her. She tried to ignore the dimple in his cheek.

"Can we talk?" She asked.

"Of course, shall we sit down?" Tom asked. He placed the empty glasses on the bar and returned to the booth table, indicating for Sandy to sit down, which she did. "What's happened?"

"Ignatius Potter's been charged. Murder and attempted murder."

"Wow," Tom said, raising his eyebrows at the news.

"It doesn't feel right," Sandy said. "I still don't think it's him."

"I admit it's strange he hung around both times if he did it," Tom said. "What are you thinking? What can I do to help?"

Sandy's stomach flipped at his offer and she reminded herself again that his interest was in catching a killer in the village, not in her.

"Did Gus turn up?" Sandy asked, lowering her voice as a couple walked in the pub hand in hand.

Tom frowned. "Last I heard, no. I asked Poppy to let me know as soon as he turns up."

"Did you tell the police?"

Tom looked down at the table. "No."

"Tom!"

"I know I'll have to, Sandy, but he's family. I can't do that to Poppy unless I have real proof."

"Right," Sandy said, standing up from the plush maroon leather of the seat.

"Where are you going?" Tom asked.

"To find proof. Nobody around here seems to care that the wrong man is being charged!" Sandy shouted, as she spun on her heels and walked out of the pub. She was trembling with anger as she walked. In the few minutes she had been in the pub, the skies had finally opened with the storm that had been threatening all day, and heavy rain soaked her skin.

"Wait!" Tom called, and she heard him running behind her. She slowed her pace but didn't stop. He caught up easily. "Where are you going?"

"To see if he's back yet." Sandy said, walking past the police station and turning right on to Water Lane. The Sanders terraced house stood in complete darkness, but then it had the last time they had visited. "Why are the lights never on?"

Tom sighed. "No reason. It's not because there's a fugitive hiding in there if that's what you're thinking."

Sandy's cheeks flushed. The thought had crossed her mind.

"Shall I?" Sandy asked, gesturing to the door with an eyebrow raised. Tom groaned and knocked at the door himself.

They stood at the door for almost five minutes before Poppy opened the door. Her hair was scraped back from her face and she wore casual fleecy joggers and an oversized t-shirt.

"You've been crying?" Tom asked, giving her a hug as she held the door open for them.

"Do you two come as a pair now?" Poppy asked, and Sandy watched as Tom's cheeks reddened.

"Your brother's helping me try and solve the murder case."

"What do I have to do with that?" Poppy asked, her voice shaky. The three of them stood in the hallway. Poppy made no suggestion that they move through into the living room.

"We need to tell the police at some point that Gus went missing on the night of the murder. I wanted to come and check he hasn't got home yet."

Poppy swallowed and looked down at her outfit. "Do I look like a woman whose husband is home?"

Sandy tried not to smile at the question. It was such an old-fashioned idea, that a wife should always look her best for her husband. Poppy Sanders was traditional, though.

"Where do you think he is?" Sandy asked.

"I don't want to know where he is." Poppy said, and Sandy realised she was a woman choosing to live in the dark in more way than one. "He'll be back, he always is."

"He's never stayed away like this before," Tom said.

Poppy laughed. "I don't tell you everything Gus does wrong, Tom. Why would I, when it's so clear you've never liked him."

"I don't dislike him," Tom muttered. "I just don't think he's right for you."

"He's been away for nearly a whole day now, Poppy. Aren't you worried?" Sandy asked.

"He's a grown man." Poppy said. "He'll be fine."

"Ok," Sandy said, realising they were unlikely to find anything else out from Poppy. "Well, if he turns up, will you let us know?"

"Of course." Poppy said. She watched from the hallway as Sandy and Tom let themselves out of the house, leaving her in the darkness.

They stood on the pavement outside for a few moments.

"You know, if we are working together on this, I should probably get your number," Tom said, flashing her a nervous smile.

"Of course," Sandy said, pulling her phone from her bag. A message flashed on the screen and she read it. "Oh my goodness!"

"What is it?"

"Derrick's woken up!" Sandy said, surprised to feel tears prick at her eyes. She decided not to fight them and allowed herself to sob. Tom wrapped his arms around her and pulled her in for a hug.

"That's amazing. Do you want to go to the hospital?"

Sandy pulled away, wiped her eyes and shook her head.

"He's got Cass and Olivia there at the moment and his mum's on her way. I'll go later. Come on, we have somewhere else to go now."

"We do?" Tom asked.

"Follow me," Sandy instructed, leading him back on to the High Street and across the village square. Gus' butchers was still in darkness, exactly as Tom had described it from earlier. Sandy peered in the window at the empty counter and the meat-cutting machinery.

Gus, like her, was a committed small business owner, and his shop was open no matter the day or the weather. Sandy had questioned him once on his decision to open on the weekdays when many of the village shops closed.

"I can open and maybe sell some meat or close and definitely sell none." He had explained with a shrug, and the simplicity of his words had helped her make the decision to extend her own opening days.

"I have an uneasy feeling about this," Sandy said.

"The whole thing's not right," Tom admitted.

"Do you have a key?" She asked.

Tom shook his head. "I don't know if anyone else does."

"Hmm." Sandy contemplated. "How do we get to the back?"

"This way," Tom said, leading her past Rob Fields' small cottage and down Church Street, the tiny lane that separated the church from the vicar's cottage. At the back of the cottage was a small unlaid path leading to the backs of the houses and shops that looked out over the village green, including the butchers. The path was unlit and as the two of them walked down it, their eyes adjusted to the growing darkness.

"It's this one," Tom said, indicating the back of the first

building after the vicar's cottage. Sandy looked and was surprised to see a light on at the back.

"What's that room?" She asked.

"I don't know," Tom admitted. "I don't make a habit of coming around here."

"Come on, let's take a look," Sandy said, and they walked carefully through the back gate and down the path to the building. Sandy hesitated a moment and in that moment Tom pushed past her and looked in the lit-up window, diving back immediately and turning to the back door, trying the handle desperately and then slamming into it with all of his weight.

"What's wrong?" Sandy asked as the door gave way on Tom's third slam into it.

"He's in here," Tom called, bursting into the building. Sandy watched as Tom darted into the room with the light on. Gus was lying on the floor, unconscious. An empty bottle of whisky lay by his side.

"Shall I call an ambulance?" Sandy asked, kneeling down next to Tom.

"Not yet." Tom said, as he gave Gus a shake.

"I don't think you should -"

"I've seen him like this before." Tom murmured, then moved close to Gus' face and shouted at him, "Wake up!"

To Sandy's surprise, Gus rolled over, sat up slightly, and promptly threw up on the floor.

"Is he -" She began to ask.

"Drunk. Bloody drunk!" Tom said, shaking his head.

Gus groaned, then opened his eyes. "What are you - you two - doing here?"

Sandy didn't know whether to be angry or disgusted with him. "What are you doing here, that's the question. You've been missing since yesterday, where have you been?"

"Having a party." Gus said with a shrug, indicating the room. Sandy saw to her surprise that every nook and cranny of the room was stashed with alcohol. Glints of tall cans flashed in between cupboards, another bottle of whisky stood atop the large fridge, a crate of cans was shoved underneath the cutting table. Sandy had never seen a sadder room in her life.

"Doesn't look like much of a party." Tom said.

"Another squatter was ran over last night." Sandy said. "You threatened to kill them all, and then one of them was ran over."

"Woah." Gus said, and Sandy saw the genuine surprise on his face. "Another murder?"

"No." Sandy said, her voice stern. "He's just woken up actually. So, whoever ran him over, he'll be able to tell us."

"Where were you last night?" Tom asked.

"You don't think it were me, do you?" Gus asked, attempting a bitter laugh and descending into a coughing fit instead.

"You disappeared." Tom said. He was sitting on the cold stone floor of the building, watching his brother-in-law carefully.

"I just had a drink. And then another. And then another. I needed to sleep it off."

"Why not just go home?" Sandy asked.

"I promised Poppy I'd cut down." Gus admitted. "The problem is, the more I think I can't have it, the more I want it. So after a few last night, I thought I'll have a good blow out, get it out of my system, like."

"He's telling the truth." Tom said. "He's an awful liar. If he'd done it, I'd know."

Sandy nodded her agreement. She had seen the surprise on his face.

"Which one of them was it?" Gus asked.

"It was Derrick, the boy who works for me."

"Ah no." Gus said, burying his head in his hands. "He's a good lad. Never seen him react badly. Even when that woman was screaming at him, he just let her have her say."

Sandy's ears pricked up. "Woman?"

14

"I'll give you a lift." Tom offered as they left the Sanders house. Tom had fetched his car and together the two of them had bundled Gus into the back seat and drove him home.

Poppy had kept them waiting for ten minutes before she opened the door, in which time the lights had been turned on and she had changed into a dress and let her hair fall free around her face. The woman's devotion to her husband made Sandy smile to herself.

"Oh, Gus." She had said, allowing Tom to help the man to the settee. Tom and Sandy had looked at each other, and left Poppy to work her magic on helping her husband recover from the hangover from hell.

"She's a special lady, your sister," Sandy said as she climbed into the passenger seat of Tom's car.

"So are you," Tom said, staring straight ahead as he spoke. "Nobody else is trying to solve this case like you are."

Sandy shrugged. "Anton Carmichael came to me for help, and I turned him away. The least I can do for him, and Derrick, is make sure the right person is punished."

"You really think you know who it is now?" Tom asked.

Sandy nodded. "I was never totally convinced of it being Ignatius Potter or Gus Sanders. This time, I'm sure."

"Well, I'm sure Anton's looking down and thanking you," Tom said.

Sandy nodded and forced herself to look out of her window as tears welled up in her eyes. She remembered Anton's appearance in the bookshop, how he had looked so carefully at the poetry collection that she had since removed and taken home with her. She rarely liked poetry but had committed to reading the book for Anton.

"Do you think they'll be ok?" Sandy asked as they pulled into the hospital car park.

"Poppy will make sure they are," Tom said, flashing Sandy a winning smile. "Do you mind if I come in with you? I want to make sure you get home safe. I'll stay in the waiting area."

"Sure," Sandy said, liking his company, liking the feel of his presence near her. "Thank you."

**

Derrick's room was on the fourth floor, and it was a hub of activity.

Sandy could see through the window that Cass and Olivia were in the room, Olivia holding hands with Derrick and chatting. Cass turned around, spotted Sandy, and waved. She got up from her chair and appeared in the corridor.

"Isn't it amazing?" She exclaimed, watching the scene in the room through the window like Sandy and Tom were.

"How's he doing?" Sandy asked. Derrick's eyes were open and he was staring at Olivia as she chatted to him.

"He's tired. Even more tired since we turned up. Olivia's telling him everything that's happened. Everything she's eaten or felt like eating but didn't! He's just listening to it all."

"What are the doctors saying?"

"Not much, you know what doctors are like. But if I read between the lines, I think he's over the worst of it now and could make a full recovery."

"That's amazing," Sandy said, grinning.

"Oh, Mrs. Deves, this is Sandy Shaw," Cass said as a short woman with curly hair and freckles pushed open the door to Derrick's room. "She's the one Derrick works for."

To Sandy's surprise, Mrs. Deves sobbed as soon as she saw Sandy, then grabbed her with both hands and forced her into a hug.

"Thank you." Mrs. Deves whispered, her breath rasped with tears. "Thank you for giving my boy a chance."

"He's an amazing young man," Sandy said, meaning every word. "I'm lucky he gave me a chance!"

"He's coming home straight from here." Mrs. Deves said, pulling back from the intense hug. "I've got my boy back."

"He's excited to get home," Sandy said.

"I'm never letting him out of my sight again." Mrs. Deves said. "Well, apart from when he comes to work, of course. I always taught him to help at home."

"He's like a machine washing dishes," Sandy said, wanting the woman to know how impressed she was with her son.

"Least I did something right then." Mrs. Deves whispered, watching Derrick through the glass. Sandy pretended not to hear the remark, suspecting it hadn't been said for her ears.

"You go in, Sandy," Cass said, giving her arm a squeeze.

"Oh yes, go on love." Mrs. Deves agreed.

Sandy smiled at them and opened the door. The room was dark, with various machines flashing lights. Olivia turned to see Sandy and stopped talking. She had been in the middle of telling Derrick something about whether or not toast should have crusts.

"I need the toilet," Olivia said, sounding young. "Can you stay with him, Auntie Sandy?"

"Of course," Sandy said, averting her eyes as Olivia placed a delicate kiss on Derrick's forehead. Only when the door closed did she look up, and stand to plant her own kiss on his cheek.

"Hello." He said, his voice croaky and dry.

"Hey, you. We've been so worried about you." Sandy said, trying not to allow her voice to choke up. "You need to take more care crossing the road."

He flashed a weak smile at her. "Mum's here."

"I just met her. She's very proud of you, Derrick. We all are."

"Fastest pot washer in the West." He said, struggling over the length of the sentence. Sandy laughed.

"Did you see who did this to you?" She asked.

Derrick shook his head, his breathing still laboured from speaking.

"You must have seen something." She pressed, desperate for anything to confirm that she was right about the identity of the killer.

Derrick shook his head again.

"Ok, let's talk about something else. Should toast have crusts or not?" Sandy teased, but Derrick's expression was serious.

"I saw." He said, each word an effort.

"If I ask you questions, can you nod or shake your head for me?" Sandy asked.

"Yeah." Derrick agreed.

"Was it a woman?" She asked.

15

*W*hen Sandy returned to Books and Bakes the next morning, she was met by a very concerned Bernice and Coral, who each stood behind the counter with their arms folded when they noticed her outside the door.

"This looks ominous," Sandy said, letting herself in and hanging her yellow mac on the coat stand.

"We're worried about you," Bernice said.

"You disappeared yesterday," Coral said.

Sandy groaned. "I'm sorry, you're right."

"You were digging around into the murder weren't you?" Coral asked. "You need to be careful, Sandy. You could make yourself the next target."

"There won't be any more targets," Sandy said. She was certain of that.

"How do you know?"

"It's simple - the murderer wanted to get the squatters away from the Manor. And they've done that."

"I'm sure someone who has already killed would do it again to stop them being caught," Bernice mumbled.

"Look, I appreciate your concern, I do, but I'm safe."

"Sandy, you think everything is nice like you are, but you need to be careful," Coral said. Sandy had always been naive. She remembered the time the fair had come to town when she and Coral had been teenagers, and their mum had taken them to see the rides. Money was tight so they couldn't go on anything, but Sandy hung over the rails watching the tame rides race by. She had realised at one point that people from her school had also been there, riding the dodgems and the waltzer, and then climbing off and throwing up. She had laughed to Coral about how the rides were too gentle to make people be sick, and would always remember the absolute shock she had felt when Coral had told her they were being sick because they were drunk, not just because of the ride itself. Underage drinking had shocked Sandy and for weeks afterward, she had wondered how she could not see something so obvious.

"Ignatius Potter has been charged." Sandy said. "Do you really believe he's the killer? Because if you don't, it's down to the rest of us to find out who the real killer is."

Bernice shifted uncomfortably. "I don't think it's Ignatius Potter."

"Well, neither do I," Coral admitted. "But that's for the police to worry about."

"The police aren't worried about it," Sandy explained. "That's the problem. I've spoken to DC Sullivan. His case is closed. He's probably on his way back to the city after he's taken Derrick's statement."

"Derrick's awake?" Coral asked, clasping a hand over her mouth.

Sandy nodded. "That's why I didn't come back yesterday, I heard from Cass that he had woken up so I went to visit him."

"How is he? Can we visit?" Bernice asked.

"He's tired, but I think he will be okay. I met his mum."

"What's she like?" Coral asked. "I can't imagine what kind of mother would let their child become homeless."

"She didn't let him," Sandy said. "He crept out one night and the first she knew where he was was when he rang to tell her he'd got a job and would be going home soon."

"Wow." Coral breathed.

"Now, come on, we've got work to do. I appreciate your concern, but I have to finish this. I'm too close to give up."

"You know who did it, don't you?" Coral said, always able to interpret her little sister's expressions or tones of voice.

"Yes," Sandy said. "I do."

**

Sandy spent the whole day upstairs, tending to the books and setting up the new till she had ordered so she could serve book customers away from the cafe.

She was glad of the peace and quiet, which allowed her to plot how she would confront the killer.

Whenever nerves crept into her mind, she thought back to Derrick's laboured breathing and his mother's sobs. She had to sort this - for them.

To keep her busy, she sorted through some of the boxes of new stock that had arrived over the last week and had been sat neglected in the upstairs storeroom. Sandy bought new second-hand stock from house clearances, auctions and even online auctions. A fresh supply of books was one of the best ways for her shop to encourage repeat customers.

The boxes in the storeroom had been purchased a fortnight ago from a house clearance 100 miles away. She had given up a Sunday to travel across and view the books, offering the elderly homeowner a fair price and refusing his offer to help her trudge the books down his path and load them into the boot of her Land Rover.

Opening new boxes of books was one of Sandy's favourite things to do and something she had been less able to do when the books had been cramped into the small portion of the cafe area downstairs.

As soon as she opened the books, the smell hit her. The man had been a keen historian and these books had a history of their own, being sourced over a period of decades from around the world. They were unusual, specialist titles, and they would sell well.

Sandy had learned that the more unusual a book was, the better it would sell. She couldn't compete with the prices that the supermarket chains offered new releases for, so rarely stocked those items. Instead, she could spend the time and energy on finding valuable collections or large discount deals, and focus on those.

She gave each book a wipe with a dry tea towel as she pulled them from the boxes, then wrote out a price sticker and stuck it over the ISBN on the back cover.

As much as her team were excellent bakers and great salespeople, pricing books was a job only she could do. She had spent countless hours learning the skill by studying what her competitors priced their books at and even attending bookseller conferences, long before her dream of owning a bookstore had become reality.

"Excuse me?" A voice called from the till. Sandy stood up, noticing again how she had to use her hands to push her bottom up and gain enough momentum to stand, and walked out of the storeroom to see Rob Fields with an arm full of books. "Ah, hello Sandy, can I pay up here now?"

"You'll be my guinea pig to see if the till works." Sandy said with a laugh. "Let's give it a whirl."

"I'm game," Rob said, placing the pile of books on the counter.

"Treating yourself?" Sandy asked, spotting more books on watercolour painting and an old Bible amongst the pile.

"I am," Rob admitted. "And it's always good to support a local business, of course."

"Of course." Sandy agreed. She was thrilled for any locals to consider it their civic duty to buy books from her shop. "I'd have thought you'd have had a Bible already, Rob."

"Very amusing." He said with a smile. "I like the old ones, they're so beautifully made."

Sandy nodded. "So many people like to collect things, don't they."

Rob shrugged. "It's one of our many weaknesses as humans. We value the inanimate... more than our fellow living creatures, at times."

"Yes," Sandy said. "We've seen that with the hit and runs."

"I hear young Derrick is recovering. I've been praying for him."

"Thank you," Sandy said. "He's a good lad."

"Everyone's good, Sandy," Rob said. "Even the person doing the hit and runs, in their mind, they'll be doing good. I also hear you think you know who's done it?"

Sandy's face blanched of colour. She didn't want that news making its way around the village. She gave an awkward laugh.

"I've had a few guesses, that's all." She said, downplaying it.

"Hmm," Rob said, handing over the money for his

books, which Sandy had placed in a large carrier bag. "Don't worry about the change."

"Thank you," Sandy called, putting the 30p change into the tips jar next to the till. She watched Rob Fields walk away and then returned to the storeroom to continue her opening, wiping and pricing of the new stock.

She had been sure that with enough time, and peace, a plan to confront the killer would have occurred to her, but as the sky grew dark and the constant throng of customers faded away to a trickle, she still had no inspiration.

She sat cross-legged on the floor and pulled out a book about the history of stately homes, wiping it absent-mindedly.

Rob Fields' words rang through her mind.

Even the person committing the hit and runs was doing good in their own mind.

And from nowhere, she knew what she had to do, and whose help she needed.

---

16

*B*ernice and Coral had eyed her when she suggested they leave the cleaning up to her and head home when the shop closed for customers, but she insisted that after their help running the shop, it was her turn to help them.

They hadn't needed any more convincing. Washing the dishes at the end of a busy was everyone's least favourite job.

They had bundled themselves back into their scarves and coats and bid her good night, and Sandy had watched them go, then left the dirty dishes and headed back upstairs.

Her text to Dorie had been sent almost an hour earlier, and Sandy could picture the news being spread throughout the village.

She sat on the floor in the storeroom and waited.

And listened.

She knew it was a risky plan, but she could think of no other ideas.

She had told Dorie, the village's biggest gossip, that she knew who the real killer was and would present her evidence to the police the next morning, after working late in the bookshop all night.

The real killer would have to try and stop her.

She tried to control her nerves as she considered the danger she had placed herself in.

She was almost tempted to run downstairs and lock the door, but as she pushed herself up, she was sure she heard a noise.

Every hair on her body stood on edge as a chill ran through her. She took a gulp and picked up the only thing resembling a weapon, the large and heavy till.

As she stood still, her heartbeat deafening in her chest, she saw a dark shape creep up the staircase and into the room. The figure looked around but didn't seem to notice her; they must need time to adjust to the darkness.

Sandy recognised this as her chance to strike but found that she was frozen to the ground. The shape spotted her then and moved towards her, and as they advanced, Sandy realised who it was.

"Tom?" She asked in surprise.

"What the hell are you doing?" He whispered, taking the till from her hands and placing it back on the counter. "The whole pub's talking about your message to Dorie. How could you be so foolish?"

"Tom, I -" Sandy began.

They both jumped at the sound of a large crash from downstairs. Sandy gazed at Tom and he gazed back at her.

"What do we do now?" Tom asked.

"Leave it to me," Sandy said. "I have to be alone, go in the storeroom."

Tom moved away from her and disappeared into the shadows of the storeroom.

"And leave that bloody till alone, it's too heavy to be any protection. You'd be better off with a big book." Tom hissed.

Sandy looked around her, not wanting to take her eyes away from the staircase. She bent down to the ground, keeping her gaze on the stairs, and picked up a large coffee table book that a customer had changed their mind about purchasing earlier in the day. Sandy had left it behind the counter planning to return it to the right shelf and then forgotten about it.

The book felt hard and heavy in her hands, but she was much more able to move her arms - and her whole body - while holding it. She stood back up and took a deep breath as a shadow appeared on the staircase.

Sandy moved to the till so that the counter was placed between her and the person. The shape was small, but Sandy knew they were also deadly.

She let out a small cough, deciding she would prefer the person to make their attack on her from in front of her. She didn't think her heart would withstand a game of hide and seek in the dark space.

"Sandy." The voice came, as the person advanced towards her. The accent confirmed her suspicions. "I hear you've solved the case."

"I have an idea," Sandy said, hoping the person couldn't hear the tremble in her voice as much as she could. "Are you here to tell me I'm wrong?"

The woman laughed. "I'm here to persuade you it's better not to speak to the police."

"Persuade me how?" Sandy asked.

"Peacefully - I hope." The woman said.

Sandy took a step back and flicked on the lights, hoping that Tom had been hidden away from the door of the storeroom. She attempted to make her face as stern and fearless as she could as she met Pritti Sharma's gaze.

"Why did you do it?" Sandy asked.

Pritti laughed, her attractive face contorted in exasperation. "You know why."

"I'd like to hear it from your side because I think you think you were doing the right thing."

"Have you ever read my work contract?" Pritti asked.

Sandy shook her head.

"I don't have one," Pritti explained. "My family have worked for the Harlows for three generations. My earliest memories are of my mother in their kitchen, making their meals. I'd sit on the floor playing with a rag doll, keeping quiet until my mother had met all their needs and it was time for us to return home."

"The Harlows appreciate everything your family has done for them," Sandy said, as Pritti edged closer to her.

"Of course they do. I know that. I knew before I could speak that I would work for them too, just as my daughter will take over from me. My father taught me to be loyal to the Harlow family over every other person, even our own family, as they were the reason we had food on our table."

"Your father didn't work?"

Pritti snorted, her nostrils flaring. "He was ill. He let my mother work, just as my husband lets me work."

"Is this about your job? Did you think the Harlows wouldn't return if the Manor was damaged?"

"Of course not!" Pritti said. "Did you hear what I said about loyalty? I choose them. Always. I choose them before myself."

"What was it, then? Help me understand." Sandy said.

"Charlotte Harlow embarrassed her family," Pritti explained, referring to Charlotte's conviction for the murder of Reginald Halfman. "She brought shame on them because she put her own desires ahead of her family's. She could have inherited everything, the foolish girl. I saw the shame on their faces as they left, Sandy. And then the squatters arrived and everyone was gossiping about the Harlows again. I couldn't bear it."

"I don't think people were gossiping, Pritti. Everyone cares about the Harlows."

"Huh!" Pritti exclaimed. "Where were you, then? Where were you when Charlotte was taken away in a police car? Where was everyone when the squatters came?"

"Where were you?" Sandy asked.

"I was at the Manor every single night, tidying up their mess, telling them to leave, making sure they knew they weren't wanted. They didn't pay any attention to me. And then you turned up with food for them! Why would they ever leave if they were being fed and kept dry?"

"They're people, Pritti, just like me and you."

"And I didn't want to have to hurt them. They left me no choice." Pritti said. "But the problem is resolved now. They've gone, we can all move on."

"You know I can't let that happen," Sandy said.

As she spoke, she sensed a movement behind her and saw DC Sullivan appear from his pre-arranged hiding place of an aisle of books. Pritti glanced from Sandy to the police officer, then reached into her handbag and pulled out a gun.

"Get down!" DC Sullivan called, and Sandy dived behind the counter. She saw a flash of movement as Tom appeared from the storeroom and raced across towards Pritti, a few feet behind DC Sullivan.

Sandy covered her eyes as she heard a single shot of the gun and a thud on the floor, then forced herself to calm her breathing and peer around from the counter.

Pritti lay motionless in a dark pool, with DC Sullivan reaching for his radio and calling for help. Tom hung back, still on his feet, his skin almost translucent it was so pale.

DC Sullivan pressed two fingers against Pritti's neck, keeping them in place for what felt like an age, before glancing first at Tom and then at Sandy.

"She's dead." He pronounced.

17

*B*ooks and Bakes had to be closed for several days following Pritti's suicide, and Sandy used the rare break as a chance to catch up on her reading. She spent a whole day nestled underneath her duvet in bed chain-reading a series of four small mystery novellas. She even made cheese on toast for lunch and ate that in bed too! The day felt naughty and well-earnt.

By the second day, she was missing her routine and feeling bored, so headed into her small kitchen and looked through her favourite recipe book. There was a recipe for an avocado lemon cake she had wanted to try for ages, and she decided today was the day.

The recipe was simple, requiring just five ingredients for the cake itself, and in Sandy's opinion, the simplest recipes were the best.

She switched on the oven to 170 degrees and pulled out her trusty loaf tin, which had been her mother's. Then, she turned the radio on and grabbed her electric mixer, then beat together four eggs and a cup of sugar until the mixture became light and fluffy.

Sandy cut two avocados out of their peel and discarded the stones, then measured out a cup of avocado, deciding to continue her indulgent break and popping the remaining avocado in her mouth. In a second bowl, she mashed the avocado, then sifted in 2 cups of flour and one and half teaspoons of baking powder.

The avocado mix was added to the sugar and egg mixture, and folded gently, before the whole mixture was poured into the loaf tin and cooked for 45 minutes.

While the cake was cooking, Sandy made herself a mug of steaming hot mocha and curled up in her favourite armchair in the living room.

"This is the life." She said aloud to herself, as she picked up her mug to take the first sip.

"Sandy!" A voice came from outside, and to Sandy's surprise, Tom Nelson's face appeared at her window. She tried not to jump, but she had been on edge ever since the showdown with Pritti Sharma.

She padded through to the hallway and unlocked the door, letting Tom in.

"Didn't you hear me?" He asked. She stared at him. "I've been knocking."

"Oh!" Sandy exclaimed, leading him to the living room. "I was in the kitchen."

Tom took a sniff. "Something smells good."

"Avocado lemon cake."

"Sounds... interesting."

"I've never tried it before," Sandy said. "I needed something to keep me busy. I'm not used to having all this free time."

"That's kind of why I'm here," Tom said, and his cheeks flushed. "I'm free until 6 tonight, I wondered if you fancy going off somewhere. Together, like. With me."

"Would it be a -" Sandy began.

"A date? Well, I'd like it to be if you would." Tom said, flashing her the grin that revealed his dimple.

"I'd like that," Sandy admitted, feeling her stomach flip with excitement. "I should warn you, I'm stubborn sometimes."

"Yeah, I'd already worked that out," Tom said, with a laugh.

"I need to let this cake bake, do you want a drink before we head out?" Sandy offered.

"Sure, can I get a black coffee?" Tom asked, then stood up from the settee. "In fact, why don't I make it?"

"It's fine, I'm missing making drinks for people, so let me," Sandy said. She padded through into the kitchen, the avocado cake giving off a glorious smell, and boiled the kettle again.

She thought of Pritti Sharma's children and husband, who had been the only people to attend her funeral, and decided to take the finished cake to them. She had no idea what kind of reception she would receive from them, and she didn't condone Pritti's crimes, but something the woman had said stood out for Sandy.

The Harlows had fled the village because of the shame they felt that their daughter had committed awful crimes. What if an act of friendship from Sandy, or another villager, could have shown the Harlows that they didn't need to leave their home?

"Here you go," Sandy said, placing the drink on the coffee table in front of Tom. She still blushed whenever his gaze met hers. She'd have to learn to stop that.

"Thanks! So, where shall we go today?"

"I'd like to run a couple of errands if you don't mind?

Then we could do something nice together after?" Sandy said.

"I can be your chauffeur for your errands, ma'am." Tom offered, and Sandy grinned and nodded her head.

**

It turned out that the Sharma house was next door to Gus and Poppy Sanders, something that neither Sandy nor Tom had known.

"I knew there were kids next door, I've heard them playing sometimes but never seen who they were."

"Wish me luck," Sandy said, as she opened the passenger door of Tom's car. The avocado lemon cake sat on her lap, still warm from the oven.

As she opened the gate, she noticed a small face peering at her from behind the net curtain up at the window. She gave a smile and a small wave, wanting to signal she was visiting as a friend.

She knocked on the door and heard the shuffling of feet within.

After a wait that was long enough to cause her to begin feeling anxious, the door opened, and Sandy stood face to face with a man she assumed must be Pritti's husband - now her widower.

"Mr. Sharma?" She asked. The man was small and appeared too frail for his age. His back was bent over and a stick supported his weight. The boy and girl who had been with Pritti just recently in Books and Bakes peeked from behind their father. "I'm Sandy, I knew Pritti."

Mr. Sharma made a small noise from in his throat, like a sob desperate to escape. "How can I help you?"

"I brought a cake," Sandy said, thinking how feeble the words sounded given what the family was going through.

"For us?" Mr. Sharma asked. "Nobody else has been. The police say my wife did terrible things, I don't know what to think."

Sandy saw the confusion in his eyes and wanted more than anything to scoop him into a hug. "Mr. Sharma, I knew your wife. She did do very terrible things, but you and your children have done nothing wrong. I wanted you to know you're in my thoughts."

The man nodded, as if struggling to take in so many words after so much silence.

"If I can do anything, let me know," Sandy said.

"Yes." The man said, still appearing in a daze.

"Can one of the children take the cake?' Sandy asked, smiling at the boy and girl. Their outfits were mismatched and their hair appeared unbrushed. She imagined that Mr. Sharma would be learning to do many things for the first time now his wife was gone.

"I will!" The girl volunteered, squeezing past her father and taking the cake from Sandy's hands. Sandy had transferred it out of her beloved loaf tin and wrapped it in tin foil.

"It has nuts on top, can you all eat nuts?" Sandy asked. The girl nodded, her dark eyes wide in wonder.

"Ok. I'll be going. I hope you're all ok." Sandy said, as she raised her hand and gave a little wave, then turned and walked away from the house. As she climbed into the car, Mr. Sharma remained at the door watching her, still looking confused.

"How did that go?" Tom asked. "It looked a little, strained?"

"I think the man's still in shock," Sandy said, fastening her seatbelt.

"Poor family," Tom said. "Right, next stop, ma'am?"

Sandy laughed. "The hospital please, driver, and be quick!"

**

Derrick was in the hospital reception when they arrived, sat in a cosy armchair with Olivia stood by his side, her hand in his.

He gave a huge smile when he saw Sandy and attempted to stand.

"Stop!" She scolded. "I'll bend down to you."

She reached down and planted a kiss on his cheek, taking in the scent of aftershave and disinfectant. "How are you feeling?"

"Glad to be leaving this place." He admitted. "They've been good to me, but it's time to get home."

"You can say that again." Mrs. Deves said, appearing at the side of Sandy. "Taxi's not here yet, son."

"They're always late." An old man called as he hobbled past them.

Sandy smiled at him.

"We can give you a lift home?" She offered, glancing at Tom who nodded his agreement.

"It's alright love, we've rung for it now." Mrs. Deves said.

"Are you going back with them, Olivia?" Sandy asked.

"Yeah, I want to see where he lives since I'll be visiting him for a bit." Olivia said. Sandy nodded.

"I'll be back at work as soon as I can, I promise, lady." Derrick said. "If you still want me, that is?"

"Of course I do!" Sandy exclaimed. "Although the shop's closed at the moment."

"Yeah, we heard about that. Terrible business. She shot herself?"

Sandy nodded, remembering the gunshot and the thud of a body hitting the ground. As desperate as she was to return to work, she was nervous about seeing her beloved first floor again.

"Poor woman," Derrick mumbled, and his words brought Sandy back to the present.

"Poor woman? She tried to kill you, Derrick." Mrs. Deves said, keeping an eye out of the glass-fronted wall for their taxi.

"I know. Imagine how mad you have to be to do what she did. She needed help."

Sandy nodded.

Pritti had been doing the right thing, in her head. And that was the danger. Nobody seeks help to talk them out of doing something they know is right.

"Well, I wanted to come and see you." Sandy said. "We'll leave you guys to it. See you soon, Derrick."

"See you, lady," Derrick called, lifting his hand to give a weak wave.

**

"Shall we go to The Tweed?" Sandy asked as she climbed in the passenger side of Tom's car.

"The Tweed? Don't you want to go somewhere more, private?" He asked.

"Not really," Sandy admitted. "I'm happy to let you show me off."

Tom burst into a grin and drove back towards Waterfell Tweed, parking the car outside the pub. He held the car door, and the pub door, open for Sandy and she thought to herself how she could get used to being spoilt by him.

The pub was quiet, and they took a seat in a booth closest to the roaring log fire.

"What do you want?"

"I'll have a glass of white wine," Sandy said. It was rare that she drank alcohol, but this felt like a special occasion.

"Perfect," Tom said. He went to the bar and ordered the drinks from Tanya, the barmaid, who looked between Tom and Sandy and burst into a smile. Sandy shook her head and smiled to herself, sure the gossip would spread around the village in no time, and not minding one bit.

"Here we go," Tom said, placing her wine in front of her and his own pint of beer in front of himself. "I hear this place does food but I don't know if I'd risk eating it."

Sandy laughed. "I've eaten in worse places, there's a really dodgy cafe just a few doors up."

"Ah yes, I heard about that. Didn't Health and Safety shut it down?"

Sandy descended into laughter, feeling the tension of the recent experiences disappearing. She looked across at Tom and raised her glass to him.

"To new friends." She suggested.

Tom raised his own pint and chinked her glass. "To new beginnings."

**

Tom turned out to be easy company.

He was interested in her, asking lots of questions and giving her his full attention as she answered. Not once did he take out his phone or appear distracted.

Sandy allowed herself to feel content, to enjoy the afternoon for what it was, and not over think what it may mean.

"Tom, tell me something very important." She asked, leaning in close to him. "Where's the best place to curl up with a book?"

Tom roared with laughter. "Are you kidding? Come with me!"

He stood up and pulled her - actually pulled her - by the hand after him, to the door that led to the private area of the pub. His home. He turned to the staircase, raised an eyebrow at her, and led her up the stairs, into a room that overlooked the village square.

"Oh my goodness!" Sandy exclaimed. The room was a library. Every wall was covered with bookcases, which were full to the brim with books of all colours and sizes. On the far wall stood an ornate fireplace, with a leather armchair on either side of it. A small coffee table stood in front of the chairs, with a selection of coffee table books arranged on it.

"You like?" Tom asked, turning in a full circle to display the whole of the magnificence of the room.

"I cannot believe this!" Sandy cried. She approached one bookcase and scanned the titles hungrily; her eyes falling on some familiar titles but many she had never heard of.

She had no idea how long she spent in the room, but Tom finally noticed the time on the old grandfather clock that stood in the corner of the room.

"I need to get down there, Tanya's shift's finishing." He said. "You can stay up here if you want?"

"Oh no, I couldn't do that," Sandy blurted, placing the book she had been looking at back on its shelf. "But I'd love to come and see it again."

"Good," Tom said, flashing his dimple-revealing smile again.

She followed him down the staircase, giving one last longing look at the library room. What a surprise the man had turned out to be.

As they appeared in the public part of the pub, a toast erupted, and Sandy thought it was people noticing that she had just emerged from the private section with Tom Nelson.

In front of her, however, stood a crowd of people, none of whom were paying attention to her and Tom. The two looked at each other quizzically, until a young dark haired man stepped back and trod on Sandy's foot.

"Ouch! Be careful." She exclaimed, making the man turn to look at her.

"Sandy Shaw!" The man exclaimed, grabbing her in a hug. He was tanned and very handsome, but young.

"Do I know you?" She asked, extracting herself from the man's grip.

"Ha! How quickly I'm forgotten!" He laughed, revealing a glass of Champagne in his hand.

"You do look a bit familiar." She admitted, but she was unable to place him.

"It's me, Sebastian!" He said, with a grin.

"Sebastian? Oh my! It's so good to see you!" Sandy said, allowing him to grab her into another hug. "Where are your parents?"

"Mingling somewhere, you know what they're like." Sebastian said, gesturing off towards the crowd in a distracted way. Sandy peered past him and spotted Benedict and Penelope a few feet away, encircled by villagers eager to welcome them home.

"So..." Sebastian said. "What have I missed?"

HONEY FOR MY HONEY

HONEY CAKE RECIPE

Ingredients:

250g clear honey, plus 2 tbsp extra to glaze
225g unsalted butter (cut into cubes)
100g dark muscovado sugar
3 large eggs, beaten
300g self-raising flour

Method:

1. Preheat the oven to gas mark 3

2. Take a 20cm cake tin - butter and line

3. Place a medium pan on the heat and add the butter cubes, honey and sugar. Allow mixture to melt over a low heat. When the mixture is all liquid, increase heat and allow to boil for 1 minute.

4. Leave honey mixture to cool for 15-20 minutes so the eggs don't cook when added in

5. Sift the flour into a large bowl

6. Beat the eggs into the honey mixture when it has cooled

7. Add the egg and honey mixture to the flour, beating to make a smooth, runny batter

8. Add mixture to the cake tin and bake for 50-60 minutes until cake has risen and springs back when touched. Cake should be golden brown.

9. Remove cake from tin and place on a wire rack.

10. Warm 2 tbsp honey and brush or drizzle over the top of the cake to create a glaze

Variations:

Try adding crushed nuts or poppyseed to the glaze or the cake mixture itself.

THANK YOU FOR READING

As an independent author, my success depends on readers sharing the word about my books and leaving honest reviews online.

If you enjoyed this book, please consider leaving an honest review on Amazon or GoodReads.

I know that your time is precious, and I am grateful that you chose to spend some of your time entering the world of Waterfell Tweed with me.

To see the the latest releases, visit:

author.to/MonaMarple

And to receive exclusive content and the latest news, join my VIP Reader List by visiting:

http://monamarple.com/vip-reader-list/

A VALENTINE'S KILL:

"His Lordship's back, all right." Dorie Slaughter said in between sips of tea. Sandy tried to withhold a smile at the older woman's gossip as she placed a bacon sandwich on the table in front of her and attempted to retreat to the counter.

"Hold on, Sandy, you want to hear this." Elaine Peters said from her seat next to Dorie.

"Oh, I'd love to, I need to finish your breakfast though," Sandy said with a smile, then speed-walked away. Her friend and employee, Bernice, was plating up mushrooms in the kitchen.

"Elaine's?" Sandy asked. Bernice nodded. They didn't get many vegetarians in Books and Bakes and the plate was missing sausage and bacon. "Don't suppose you want to take it out for me?"

Bernice wiped her hands on a tea towel and met Sandy's gaze. "Not a chance, boss."

"Boss?!" Sandy exclaimed.

Bernice laughed. "It's like a witches' coven out there, I'm staying here."

Sandy rolled her eyes but couldn't argue. Everyone who

had come to the cafe that morning had been buzzing with the excitement of some new piece of village gossip that Sandy had so far escaped hearing about. She loved Waterfell Tweed, but the villagers were like a swarm of locusts for news and rumours.

"Fine, I'll take one for the team," Sandy said, picking up Elaine's plate and returning to the noisy front-of-house.

"I thought he'd been sacked." Her sister, Coral, called across the cafe from behind the counter. Coral had joined Sandy to work the till when she had been made redundant from her job as a journalist, and she still loved digging for a new story.

"On a sabbatical," Dorie said. "What does that even mean?"

"A sabbatical... well, it's like, erm..." Elaine stumbled over her words. It was unlike Elaine to be involved in village gossip, but Sandy knew she was making an effort to spend more time with Dorie, who had been struggling with loneliness since Elaine began dating her adult son.

"Here you go, Elaine." Sandy said, placing the breakfast in front of her. Elaine grabbed the knife and fork and stabbed a mushroom, then placed it in her mouth and chewed. Her appreciative groans told Sandy she was enjoying the taste.

"Sandy, you'll know..." Dorie called as Sandy turned on her heels to walk away. "What's a sabbatical? Or maybe it was a secondment."

"It's just like a long holiday, isn't it? A few months out away from work?" Sandy said, shrugging her shoulders to show she wasn't sure.

She took a moment to survey the busy cafe and allowed herself a smile. Busy days paid the bills.

As well as Dorie and Elaine, there were at least eight

other tables bustling with people, all either tucking into food orders or reviewing the menu.

"It's not funny." Dorie scolded, and it took a moment for Sandy to realise that the woman was speaking to her. Her smile must have been wider than she intended.

"Sorry." Sandy said. She flashed a smile and then walked through the tables to the staircase at the back of the ground floor area, which she walked up into the bookshop area.

Derrick Deves sat behind the counter, still recovering from being run over by a car. He grinned as soon as he saw her. "Come up for a bit of peace?"

"What's got into everyone today?" Sandy asked, then realised that her question made her a gossip talking about gossipers. "Actually, forget I said that. I don't want to know! How's it going up here?"

"Dead easy," Derrick admitted. Sandy had realised before Derrick's injuries that she needed the upstairs till manned full-time, and with Derrick still recovering, he was the perfect person to sit there all day. "I'd rather be up and about, though."

"I know, and you will be soon. I've got a long list of jobs waiting for you." Sandy admitted. They were missing Derrick's pot-washing too, which he had done quicker than anyone else and with a happier heart.

"Glad to hear it. I don't know how people work in offices all day, sitting at a desk... it'd drive me mad."

Sandy shrugged. "You're warm and comfy, I'd take it over being a builder or something where you're outside in all weather."

"Bit of cold killed no one, lady," Derrick said. Sandy raised an eyebrow at him. "Well, yeah, I guess it can actually."

They both laughed until Sandy heard a shriek from downstairs.

Derrick was up off his chair in a shot.

"I'll go, you stay up here and rest your legs." Sandy insisted, placing a hand on his arm. She ran downstairs to see most of the customers peering out of the shop window across the village square. Coral was amongst them, gazing out, and even Bernice had poked her head out of the kitchen. Sandy met her gaze. Bernice shrugged and returned to the kitchen.

"What's going on?" Sandy asked, feeling like a teacher attempting to control an unruly class of children.

Nobody appeared to hear her. If they did, they ignored her.

"What's going on?" She repeated, louder. Coral turned and put a finger to her lips, telling her sister to shush. Sandy rolled her eyes, barged through the crowd, and opened the cafe door. The sun was unusually bright for so early in the year and her eyes struggled to focus for a second in the glare. By the time her sight had adjusted, there was nothing at all to see.

Her cafe stood on one side of the village square, looking out over the small playing field which had a well-ignored 'No Ball Games' sign standing in its middle. As she looked out, the small bus that came through the village twice a day had stopped on the opposite side of the field, and a single man was allowing his Golden Retriever to sniff his way across the field.

"What on earth's got into you lot today?" Sandy asked as she returned to the cafe.

Most of the customers had returned to their tables and several furiously sipped drinks before they cooled.

"Will someone answer me?" Sandy asked, but this question she whispered only to her sister. Her customers came in for many things, but rudeness from the owner wasn't one of them.

"He's here all right. Saw him get off the bus. Dorie got a bit overexcited, you know how she is when she's right."

Sandy definitely knew how Dorie was when she was right - intolerable. Her smugness could last for days.

"Who's here?" Sandy asked.

Coral eyed her, her brow creased with lines she wouldn't want to know were quite so visible. "Dick Jacobs! Haven't you been listening at all this morning?"

"I've been trying not to." Sandy admitted.

"Did you say Dick Jacobs?" Bernice asked, appearing from the kitchen. She smelt of gingerbread and her cheeks had a dusting of flour on them.

"Who's Dick Jacobs?" Sandy asked. She had the distinct feeling that she had been kidnapped by aliens and transported to an alternate reality overnight.

"Is he back?" Bernice asked.

"Dorie came in this morning saying he was, and we've just seen him get off the bus." Coral explained.

"Blimey." Bernice said. "I'd better check our assessments are up-to-date."

"I give up." Sandy said, holding her hands up in defeat.

"All right, Miss Dramatic, what's got into you?" Coral asked, turning her attention to Sandy as Bernice retreated into the kitchen and banged around moving lever-arch files.

"Nothing's got into me!" Sandy exclaimed in a petulant voice that she knew made it obvious something had got into her. "I don't know what any of you are talking about, that's all."

"It's fairly easy." Coral said with a sigh. "Dick Jacobs is back."

"Ah, that settles it then. Why didn't you say?" Sandy said. "Who on earth is Dick Jacobs?"

Silence fell across the cafe and Sandy turned to see most of the customers looking at her with puzzled expressions on their faces.

"You don't know Dick Jacobs?" Dorie asked.

Sandy sighed. She was tired of the whole conversation. "No, I've got no idea who he is."

"I didn't realise his sabbatical had been that long." Gus Sanders said. He was sitting at one of the far tables with his wife, Poppy. "He last came out to me, what must it have been, maybe 2 years ago... nah, must have been longer than that. Wow... time flies."

"It was four years ago, Gus." Poppy said, her voice barely a whisper. "He was against the premises being used as a butcher's, do you remember?"

"He's against everything, that bloke." Gus muttered.

"He's from health and safety, Sandy." Elaine explained.

"Everyone's getting this excited about a health and safety man?" Sandy asked, incredulous.

"He's not a health and safety man, he's the health and safety devil!" Gus said with a snigger. "I think that man dreams at night about the next business he'll close down."

"Surely, it's his job to close down businesses that shouldn't be open?" Sandy said. She couldn't imagine that health and safety officer was a popular job. Probably about as well-liked as traffic wardens. But someone had to do it.

"He'd close everyone down if he could." Dorie said. "Do you remember the wool shop?"

"The Knitting Basket?"

"That's it, thought it might be before your time. He had that place closed down because their kettle was too close to their toilet! And it was only for their own cups of tea, they didn't even serve food or drinks!"

Sandy tried to resist the temptation to roll her eyes. "I can't imagine that's the whole story, Dorie."

"You'll see, you've never been inspected by him before." Dorie said.

"What are you trying to say, Dorie?" Sandy asked, feeling her cheeks flush.

"She's right." Bernice's measured voice came from behind Sandy. Sandy turned to see that her arms were filled with lever-arch files - the records that went into running an establishment that offered food and drink to the public. Temperature checks, food rotation, cleaning records, and more. The records were thorough, accurate and up-to-date, Sandy knew. "Dick Jacobs sees it as his personal mission to close down as many businesses as he can."

Sandy could ignore the customers gossiping, but for the unflappable Bernice to issue such stark words made Sandy shiver as if someone had walked over her grave.

"Can we talk in private?" Bernice asked. Sandy nodded and followed her employee across the cafe area and upstairs to the books.

Derrick was in the middle of serving an elderly gentleman who had been browsing for at least an hour and had an arm-full of books piled on the counter.

"Dick Jacobs is bad news, Sandy." Bernice whispered. She handed the pile of folders across to her. "You need to make sure all of these are in order."

"They are in order, Bernice, we're so careful with them." Sandy said.

"He will find any tiny thing he can, and close us down. He really did close the wool shop, and he's desperate to close Gus' butchers. He's been trying to catch him out for years."

"And he hasn't managed it, doesn't that show we don't need to worry if we're doing things properly anyway, which we are?"

Bernice sighed, her lips pursed. "He has a thing against women in particular, Sandy. When he closed the wool shop down, he told Mabel that she should have been at home cleaning anyway, not trying to run a business."

Sandy felt her cheeks flush. "He really said that?"

Bernice nodded. "He wants to get the butchers closed, but I think he's scared of men. He'll be after you, after us, when he comes. It's his first visit to us, he'll want to find something. Anything."

"Ok." Sandy said. She had never seen Bernice so worried. "Ok, I'll look through these."

"Do it today." Bernice urged.

"I'll do it now." Sandy promised. There was a small office at the back of the upstairs that she never used, but which had a desk and chair left from the previous occupants.

Sandy decided to spend the rest of the morning holed up in the office, making sure that her folders would give Dick Jacobs no excuse to close her beloved business.

**

To continue reading A Valentine's Kill, order your copy now:

A Valentine's Kill
mybook.to/AVK

ABOUT THE AUTHOR

Mona Marple is a mother, author and coffee enthusiast.

When she isn't busy writing a cozy mystery, she's probably curled up somewhere warm reading one.

She lives in England with her ever-supportive husband and daughter.

Connect with Mona:
www.MonaMarple.com
mona@monamarple.com

facebook.com/MonaMarpleAuthor

twitter.com/MonaMarple

instagram.com/MonaMarple

Printed in Great Britain
by Amazon